Alex McLean
Time Traveller

Morag Ramsey

Illustrated by
John Lightbourne and Geraldine Mitchell

Seven Arches
Publishing

Published in November 2010
By Seven Arches Publishing
27, Church Street, Nassington, Peterborough PE8 61QG
www.sevenarchespublishing.co.uk

Cover design, scans and typesetting by Alan McGlynn.

Printed in Great Britain by imprintdigital.net

ISBN 978-0-9564869-0-5

To my brother Philip Worth who shares my love of Edinburgh and inspired me with his gift of improvised story telling in our childhood. He always made me the hero, and himself my trusted lieutenant.

‹IF THIS IS THE FIRST TIME YOU HAVE READ ONE OF THE BOOKS THAT RECORDS THE ADVENTURES OF CHILDREN FROM THE TWENTY FIRST CENTURY IN A TIMEZONE DIFFERENT TO TODAY. YOU NEED TO KNOW›

› That SHARP stands for The Scientific History and Art Reclamation Programme.

› That STRAP stands for the Scientific Testing and Recording of Aggression Programme.

› That time slip is something that you might suffer if you travel through time and space, in a similar way to how some people get jet lag when they fly long distances on a jet air liner.

› That if you travel through time and space you are a xrosmonaut.

CHAPTER 1

First Contact

Alex woke earlier than usual. It was six o'clock. The summer sun was already slanting through his bedroom window, but he kept his eyelids closed for as long as he could; getting up was always the hardest part of the day for Alex. But today there was a buzz of excitement at the back of his mind. What was it? Of course, it was Saturday and he was going to do the advanced climb. If all went well, he would finish the day qualified to go with the club on adult outdoor climbs. He could hardly believe that he had got this far: climbing was his passion.

About eighteen months ago Alex's dad had been made redundant. At first, when redundancy notices had been issued by his dad's firm, things were really awful. Jock, his dad, had gone from being a normal cheerful bloke, always ready to take his son out on the park to kick a football about, to a morose, grumpy guy who hardly spoke. When he did, it was to snap at those around him. Alex had taken to reading in his bedroom, sending friends long texts or sloping off to his mate Alistair's house. His mum, Maureen, had been wonderful, but even she had sometimes not been able to take it, and had answered back at an unfair jibe. Then there would be horrible rows, banging doors and icy silences for days. The odd thing was that when the redundancy actually happened, everything took a turn for the better.

First off, dad got the redundancy money. As soon as the money was there, sitting in his bank account, Jock seemed to regain his old self. He joked, laughed and chatted endlessly with Maureen about what they might spend some of it on – of course, after stashing a good bit of it away for what he called 'a wee nest egg.' Then one evening, dad called a family conference. They were big on conferences in his family, even if there were only three of them.

Apparently, dad had long held an ambition to take up rock climbing. Uncle Martin, his dad's younger brother, lived in the Highlands; he was part of a mountain rescue team. Alex realised that his dad must have been envying his brother for years.

'What do you think, Maureen?' Jock had asked his wife.

'Go for it, Jock,' his mum had said. 'You've slogged all these years and I'm more than happy to go full-time now. Remember, I'm to be upgraded to sister next month. That's going to be my real challenge… and lots more dosh!' His mum had smiled a little wickedly when she added: 'So you can be a rock-climbing house-husband till you land another job.'

Alex had watched his dad hesitate for a moment, battling with his macho pride. 'Househusband' sounded like one of those modern namby-pamby phrases that he hated. But the dream won.

'Maureen, you're a star! I'd love that. And I think so would Alex. What do you say, son?'

'Me?' Alex had queried, not really knowing what he meant.

'Yes – if I'm doing a rock climbing course, Alex, you are as well. It can be my Christmas present to you this year – I was wondering what to get you. What do you think?'

Alex had been over the moon. Now, six months on, both he and his dad had learnt a great deal about indoor rock climbing and were seriously hooked.

A sudden shout from downstairs broke into Alex's meandering thoughts.

'Alex… it's time to get up.'

'OK, Mum, I'm getting up now.' Alex stretched out, yawning. A few minutes ticked by. His mum called again:

'Alex, I know you're still in bed! Get up! Your breakfast will be ready in five minutes. I'm doing you a fry up to boost your energy levels for the climb! Don't let it spoil!'

'OK, Mum, I'm on it' Alex called down. But still he didn't move: *just one more minute,* he promised himself.

His mobile fired off under his pillow. Languidly, he dragged it out, tapped the speaker to loud and held it away from his head, expecting a message from Alistair. He looked at the screen, then shot upright in surprise. An image had emerged of a girl, about his age. She was smiling at him. Alex had never seen her before in his life!

'Sorry to wake you.'

'I wasn't asleep.'

'Good. You remember when you met with Kazaresh at the Castle Museum last week, he told you that you would be contacted, didn't he?'

'Did he?'

'You do remember, don't you?'

'No.'

'Surely your memory's not that bad!' She was laughing at him.

'My memory's just fine – I don't remember because I don't know what you're talking about. You've got the wrong person. I've never met Kaz...er... what-s'is name in my life, and the last time I was in the Castle Museum it was with my junior school doing some boring history project, and I don't think I'd be meeting any dodgy contacts with my teacher looking over my shoulder.'

The girl looked a bit worried.

'You are Danny Higgins, aren't you?'

'No, I am not. Now if you don't mind, I've a breakfast waiting for me. And anyhow, how did you get my number? Was it that idiot Alistair?' Alex was just about to close his phone when the girl said:

'Don't go. I'll not keep you long.'

Alex paused...she was a very bonnie girl.

'I've hung you in a time warp, so your breakfast won't get cold. Your mother won't notice.'

'Wha....t!? Fruit cake!!' Alex snapped off the mobile's power and stuffed it firmly under his pillow.

Then he was out of bed, shoving his feet into his slippers and pulling on his dressing gown before bounding down the short stairway that separated the first and second levels of their small flat. His mum had put his breakfast on the table in the kitchen-cum-living room.

'Smells absolutely great, Ma!'

'Did I hear you talking to someone on your phone just now?'

'Just that daft Alistair,' Alex replied through a mouthful of breakfast. Then he wondered why he had lied.

'I'm off, Alex. I'm a wee bit late for work and we're short-staffed on the ward this week. All the best with your climbing test, son. Your dad's had his break-fast and he's getting dressed now. I'll see you both later, then.' A quick peck on his head and she was fly-ing out of the house.

'Bye, Mum, thanks...' Alex called to the retreat-ing back view of his mum. Poor old ma, having to work weekends, he thought, munching happily on the sausage stuck on the end of his fork.

From his seat at the table, Alex could just glimpse through the wide window the northeast face of Edin-burgh Rock – 'E Rock' as it was called by some locals. Their flat was at the top of an old tenement block that had been converted in the eighties. The castle was just visible to the right, stunningly lit by the morning sun. Alex often daydreamed about scaling this historic rock face, but it was strictly illegal now, even more so since the work to stop dangerous rock falls had been completed only a few years ago.

As he was just about to eat his last mouthful of breakfast, a shrill ringing went off on the table. He put his fork down and traced the din to a bump under a drying-up cloth flung down behind the cornflakes packet. He snatched the cloth off. Underneath was... his own mobile! It was going off, but the sound it was making was definitely not his carefully selected ring tone!! What the heck was going on? He knew he had left it upstairs. He glared at it. Then he did a double-take. There was an additional button down the side and it was glowing red! Alex felt the hairs on the back of his neck stiffen.

He heard his dad's footsteps thundering down the stairs and looked up, expecting to see him come through the door. But he didn't; the footsteps stopped abruptly as if in mid-air, half way down the stairway, or so it seemed. At that suspended moment exactly, Alex's hand jerked across the mobile and he watched as his index finger pressed the glowing button without him meaning to do any such thing. Now fear coursed through his veins. His mouth went dry. He could scarcely breathe – he knew that something massive was about to happen. The screen was expanding, sliding away from the base and hovering in the air a metre or so away to the side. It was at least 24 inches wide, the edges defined by a small black rim. A message was appearing in black letters on the background of swirling colours:

‹Welcome, Alex McLean, to STRAP›

You can put the mobile down now. The screen will stay in place until you press the button again. My name is Korin Katanya and, as you can see, I've got your correct name this time.

Then an image appeared. It was the girl who had spoken to him that morning. Her face was there on the floating screen, smiling at him; her very pretty face framed by a mass of black curls held back by a broad silver band. Then she faded and more text appeared.

I've just managed to block you from stopping our transmission. I am sorry I alarmed and irritated you so much. I was as surprised as you were that something seemed to have gone wrong with the recruitment process. We use an agency called SHARP – a similar name to us but a different outfit – to identify suitable candidates for our Time Travel Programme. It was them who gave us the incorrect name of Danny Higgins. We knew they were a bit sloppy in their techniques, but we didn't know they were this bad! You know, you can put the phone down, as I said earlier.

Alex, as if mesmerised, carefully placed the phone on the table beside him, never taking his eyes off the floating screen. Am I dreaming? He wondered. But no, it couldn't be – there on the table beside him was the last mouthful of his breakfast cold on his plate, the packet of cornflakes, the tea towel, and of course his phone. As he looked at his phone, a sudden burst of anger flushed his cheeks.

'I left my phone upstairs in the bedroom! How did it get down here?' he shouted at the floating screen, not knowing whether he could be heard. 'And how dare you mess about with it – and what… what is this extra button?'

Clearly the girl heard him because the answer to his last question came back straightaway on the screen:

There's not just one extra button; after we've finished communicating, look at it carefully and you will see that there are three..

This information fuelled Alex's anger even more:

'What a nerve – messing about with my phone without my permission! I don't let a soul touch my phone.' But even as the words blustered out, Alex could feel his anger evaporating, giving way to the fear he had felt a moment before. After all, if this person, who ever she was, was able to stop time, what else could she do?

Then another message appeared.

I am sorry. I can see that your phone is the latest model for your time, so I know how you must feel – I love my gadgets too – but if you just listen to what I have to say, I think you will be really interested. We should have done this differently, but that can't be helped now. There is a very important reason why we have got in touch with you. I am here today to ask you to travel back in time for us. We are a scientific agency based in your future. Our work, based on very advanced scientific principles, is vital to the continued safety of the planet Earth.

Alex said nothing. The words 'travel back in time' had completely stunned him. A new message appeared.

Are you still angry?

'No. no I'm not. But who are you? Are you some weird government agency… or…or…'

No, nor are we aliens — that's what you are thinking, isn't it? And we are certainly not anything to do with your government. I am a representative of an organi-sation called STRAP — the Scientific Testing and Recording of Aggression Processes. We work mainly in war zones.

We are people from the earth's future — far into the fu-ture. We are contacting you for a very good reason, and, as I have just said, I think that when you have heard all I have to say, you'll be very interested.
Your home is on the site of a humble dwelling where a daring plot was hatched in the 14th Century. If you accept our invitation to travel back in time, you will meet the people who lived in the space of your own home in that time period. It will be a great adventure, I can assure you. Do you have any questions so far?

'Well, for starters, nobody in their right mind believes in time travel.'

I'm glad you've said that Alex. Of course, it seems very strange to you, but think about it. How is it that your dad is stuck half way down the stairs right now and is not aware of it at all. Time travel seems like fiction to you; I think in your period it was called science fiction. But then, just think what someone in the 14th century would think about your mobile phone. They would be frightened of such a device, wouldn't they? And so you are feeling frightened about what we, in our time, think of as almost commonplace. Time travel is ordinary for us – the only thing is that we can only reach back as far as the 21st century ourselves.

As I said earlier, we come from a time in the future, way in the future. It is after a terrible period that lasted a very long time called the Dark Chaos. This was when all records of humanity's history were lost in constant wars and destruction. Our science is very advanced compared to that of the twenty-first century, but for reasons too complicated to explain now, it is essential for us to find out as much about the past as possible. We need boys and girls from your time to take up the challenge, and the wonderful opportunity, to travel back in time for us.

The pause came again and Alex said quietly:
'But, why pick me, ordinary old Alex McLean, to do this time-travelling stuff?'

Well, not so ordinary, Alex. Firstly, as I said, you live right on the spot we have identified for a future project. It is possible to transport someone back to a place on the earth's surface where they have never been before, but it is much easier if the person **has** been there at some point in their lives. It's something to do with the time/space co-ordinates.

Secondly, and most importantly I might say, you're pretty good at climbing. We need someone who knows how to climb. Do you think that when we get in touch with you again and ask if you will take part in the project you might say yes?

Alex stared at the word 'climbing' on the screen and felt a thrill of excitement replace the fear. They wanted him because he could climb! He found himself saying:

'I'll…I'll think about it – yes. I'll think about it.'

That's great. Well, good luck with your test on the advanced climb today. I will contact you again in a few days. Goodbye for now, Alex. It's been great talking to you. Oh, and, by the way, don't talk to anyone about our conversation. Korin.

The screen shrank back to its normal size and settled on the surface of his phone. Then Alex heard his dad thud his way down the remaining stairs. He came through the door and appeared to have no idea that he had been suspended for quite some time. The thought tickled Alex so much, he couldn't resist grinning.

'What's so funny, son?'

'Oh…I was just thinking that Ma's filled us up with so much breakfast, I'll not manage to climb the stairs, let alone a rock face.'

'Aye, she likes to feed us men-folk up. But come on! It's almost time we set off. I'll get our sandwiches ready – you remember they said bring lunch – you sort yourself out.'

'Thanks, Dad. Give me ten and I'll be back down.'

Alex raced upstairs. He felt high with excitement. He quickly got dressed into his climbing gear and checked that he had everything he needed. Then he went back down the stairs, forcing himself to calm down; all the while the face of the girl from the future swam in front of his eyes.

CHAPTER 2

The Level Six Climb

After rushing down the flats' communal stair-way, they both ran the 200 metres or so to where the club's minibus was just pulling up. The doors swished open and the two of them, puffing and panting, climbed on board.

'Hi Jock and Alex. Were you two a bit late out of bed today?' asked Zac, the man behind the wheel, with a grin. He was a tall chap with piercing blue eyes and wisps of flyaway hair. He was their calm and very knowledgeable course leader.

'Don't know where the time went,' mumbled Jock. Mmm, thought Alex, maybe that time suspension thing did use up some of our 21st-century time.

'Well, it's a big day for you two today. Are you ready for it?'

'You'd better believe it, Zac,' said Jock.

'Can't wait,' added Alex.

'Great stuff, I'm counting on you two to keep up the club's record.' Zac, eased the gear stick in and pulled out en route to pick up the rest of the club's level-six climbers.

Jock and Alex were always the first to be picked up, so they bagged the front seats and for a short while they were the only ones on the bus except for Mary, Zac's wife. The bus began to fill quickly at its next three stops as small groups of people, all dressed for climbing, came aboard.

Despite the chatter and jokes, there was an undercurrent of excitement, with everyone keyed up to face the coming challenge. Then Zac switched on his on-board address system:

'Good morning to you all.'

Shouts of: 'Good morning, leader,' came from the occupants of the minibus.

'Today is the big day.' Zac said. 'We will be tackling what is called the 'north face' of the quarry. Its difficulty level is six, which, as you know, is as hard as it gets at the club. You've all passed the earlier levels on the indoor climbs, and well done for that, but I have no doubt that some of you will be pushed today to your strength and skill limits – so don't be disappointed if there is a request for you to repeat the level.

Zac went on and on about the time it should take, technical points to remember and safety regulations. His voice, always a bit of a hypnotic drone, lost Alex, who couldn't stop thinking about the unbelievable events of the morning. He fingered the mobile phone in his pocket and wondered how and when they had managed to add the extra buttons.

Then for some reason Zac's words broke into this thoughts. He heard:

'...standing on a massive volcanic...the castle buildings on top of the rock vary from the 14th century to the recent upgrade with the restaurant. But the first scaling of the treacherous North Face was in the 14th century, when just 20 foot soldiers and 10 or so archers and knights in the service of the Earl of Moray took the castle by stealth...' He had heard it all before in junior school.

A nudge in his back made him whip round. It was Ruth. She had moved down a few seats into the empty ones behind Jock and Alex.

'Day-dreaming again, Alex,' she teased.

'Oh I've heard it all before,' he said.

'So have I, but I'm not as rude as you as to close my eyes and apparently drop off to sleep!' Ruth gave him a cheeky grin.

Normally this would have got an angry reply from Alex. But Ruth was different. She was a year younger than him and simply the tops – probably the best climber on the bus. She was too good for him even to be jealous of her, but then her parents had climbed some of the toughest mountains in the world. The fact that Ruth came to Zac's climbing school was, Jock said, proof enough that they had chosen one of the best climbing schools in Edinburgh.

As they jumped out of the bus onto the sandy floor of the huge quarry, Alex could see another reason for choosing Zac's school: their bus had the simple words, 'South Edinburgh Indoor Climbing Club' printed on the side, whereas the minibus parked next to them was: 'Rocks Are Us.'

'Glad you didn't choose that outfit, Dad,' Alex said to Jock.

'Well naff,' agreed Jock. 'How are you feeling, Alex?'

'I'm OK, Dad – I'm fine.'

'Well, now comes the test! You take care, son.'

'You too, Dad.'

The club had been built within the huge scooped out area of the quarry. The indoor climbs were designed to provide various levels of difficulty for eight-year-olds and upwards. Now they were going to go for the only climb that was completely out in the open. For a moment, as he looked up at the ragged quarry face above him, Alex felt his stomach flip over.

Jock went with Mary and Zac to the rear of the minibus to unload ropes, pegs, and other various bits of climbing equipment. Within a surprisingly short

time they were roped together – Zac at the front, followed by Ruth, then Alex and then the other eight adults, with Mary the all-important back marker. Soon they were all feeling for their first foothold and moving along the approach ledge, itself scarily narrow.

When the climbers were a few feet off the ground, Alex felt his mind empty of all but the rock face in front of him. He was always like this. Whatever distractions filled his mind, as soon as he started to climb, he would focus. Although there was a breeze, they had only been climbing a short while before Alex felt too hot in the hard-hat; they had to wear them at all times because of health and safety regulations. Today the sweat fell into Alex's eyes and blurred his vision. With no free hand he could only brush the trickles of sweat away with the wristband of his jacket.

Halfway up, Zac allowed them to take a three minute rest, clinging to whichever ledge was nearest. The luxury of turning away from the rock face for a few moments was bliss. Then, quick as a blink, the three minutes were over.

Off and upwards again at ever-steeper angles until they reached a reinforced wall overhang. Zac had warned them of this, and one-by-one the climbers negotiated it safely. But suddenly, with a jerk, there was a tautening of the ropes that linked them. For Alex that was a first – it meant someone must have dropped off a hold! They would be dangling in mid-air! Alex glanced down briefly and spotted the figure, second from the end. Dad! Jock was struggling to regain a hand and foothold. Zac shouted down:

'Don't panic, Jock! Take a few breaths. Regain calm. The rest of you stay still, on your ledges. Jock, the link out to the overhang is to your right.

I want you to slowly feel for it… now… good… you're close… you're below it directly, five centimetres more, no, more… try again, now.'

Alex listened intently as Zac talked his dad back onto and above the tricky overhang. A cheer of encouragement went up from the others. Alex was just too fazed by the scare to join in, but huge relief swept over him as he realised Jock was OK. He focused intently on the remaining climb ahead.

At last the low boundary wall came within reach. Zac was there to clasp and high five each one of them as they came up and over at its lowest point and onto a long, low ledge which ran in a wide curve around the outer rim of the quarry.

Zac called encouragement to Dad as he helped him up and over, and all the other climbers gathered round congratulating him for regaining his calm.

'Jock, you did very well, but I'm afraid that a pass eludes you this time. But I know you'll be proud of Alex. He and Ruth are the two youngest members of the club ever to complete and pass this level-six climb, but...' Zac was interrupted as a cheer went up from the others. Alex grinned, dead chuffed... so did Jock.

'Well done, son – you've more than rescued the family honour!'

Zac smiled at them and continued: 'But, next time, Jock, I'm sure you'll make it – anyone can make the mistake you did at that particular overhang. It is only a bit more tricky than the others, but as climbers near the top, they tend to get a bit careless. It's the reason this is a level six. Total focus on the face a hundred-per-cent of the time is essential.'

Alex went up to his dad and gave him a friendly push. 'You got me worried there for a moment, Dad.'

'I was worried myself – I'm passing all climbing ambitions on to you right now. I'm not sure I ever want to see a rock face again.'

'Don't say that!'

'Just banter son, just banter!'

Zac called the club members together to let them know that they had an hour for their picnic lunch there on top of the quarry. 'But stay well clear of the closure wall', he said. 'Then you can, if you wish, abseil down, or, if faint-hearted, walk back down the steps to the minibus in the car park.

'What are you doing, Dad?'

'Oh I've had enough thrills for one day, I'll go back down the steps. I bet I know your choice.'

'Definitely – I'm abseiling down.'

'Me too,' said Ruth.

The adults scattered into two groups, leaving Alex and Ruth together. They grinned at each other a little awkwardly, and then Alex spotted a great place to eat lunch.

'Look – there's a viewing bench over there. We can eat our sandwiches without getting any spiders crawling all over them. And for starters, we can take these awful hard-hats off!'

They raced up the slope to the bench, chucking the hard-hats underneath. Ruth shook out her hair; it was light brown, cut in a short bob, and amazingly straight and shiny. She didn't have fabulous looks, but her smile lit up her whole face. Alex found himself watching for her smile.

For a few minutes they both just stood in silence staring out towards the stunning outline of the City of

Edinburgh and the Firth of Forth estuary in the distance. Then Alex broke the silence:

'We've done it! We've passed – I can't believe it!'

'I know, it was an amazing experience,' Ruth agreed, turning to smile at him and sending his stomach into a spin. 'It was such an amazing feeling – getting it right, getting to the top of such a climb; knowing you can actually scale something that looks impossible from the ground.'

'I'm glad we did this together... I mean the climb and everything,' said Alex, wanting to say more; to say that he thought she was pretty amazing and the best climber ever for her age. But he didn't.

'Nothing else could ever be this thrilling,' Ruth added.

'Mind you,' Alex grinned, turning to open up his lunch box, 'amazing sandwiches, stunning crisps and thrilling drinks... could come close!'

'Idiot!' Ruth thumped him in the chest and they both fell about laughing before starting to munch. They shared, of course: 'Can't beat variety,' Ruth commented contentedly.

The truly glorious summer weather, the light breeze off the North Sea and the thrill of having achieved an adult climb made them both high. The hour flew by, but not before they learned quite a bit more about each other.

Ruth's dad spent a good part of the year climbing in distant places all over the globe. He carried out scientific tests and gathered information for the university. Her mother used to go with him, but now stayed at home to look after Ruth and her two younger brothers, who were only seven and nine – still at primary school. Ruth had started at an exclusive girls' secondary a year ago. Alex, now nearly at the end of his second year at St Phillip's Comprehensive, felt so street-wise in comparison, especially as Ruth felt obliged to text her mum to let her know everything went well with the climb.

'Aren't you going to text *your* mum?' Ruth asked. Alex shook his head.

'It's funny how much my mum worries about me,' said Ruth. 'She used to do really dangerous stuff herself, so why is she so fussed about me?'

'Well, I expect she just worries because you're pretty young to be climbing at this level.'

'You're only a year older.'

'Makes all the difference,' Alex teased, straightening his shoulders and showing how much taller than her he was. 'Older wiser, taller, stronger!' he taunted.

'Oh you annoying boy!' Ruth aimed a punch at him and Alex dodged to the side. Then Zac started calling for those who wanted to abseil down to join him. They quickly stuffed their lunch boxes into their light back packs, picked up their hard hats from under the bench and raced over to Zac.

To Alex's surprise, he and Ruth were the only two up for abseiling. They joined Zac, who was waiting over by a sign that said: 'Out of Bounds', where there were abseiling drop ropes permanently set up, attached to a firm, flat rock platform on the edge of the quarry.

Harnessed safely into the abseiling gear and with hard-hats back on, Zac saw them launch safely into space, one-by-one. They had both done abseiling before, and so had little trouble in light-footing it down the face to the bottom. Mary was waiting for them, beaming at their faultless descent. Here were two young climbers, no doubt 'hooked for life,' she thought as she unhooked them.

'Brilliant ascent and descent, both of you. You're ready to progress to the next level, which can take you onto quite a few outdoor cliffs and mountain sites. But, of course, never go without your parents, or their approval. I'll issue you with your certificates next time you're at the club.'

'Does this mean we can scale the north face of Edinburgh Castle?' Alex asked, knowing what the reply would be.

'No, it does not! Try that and you'll have half the Edinburgh police force on your track.' Mary was about to go on about the cameras covering every section of the Rock when she realized Alex was grinning.

'You cheeky thing – you knew that already didn't you?'

'Of course he did, Mary,' said Ruth, 'it's just that all the excitement has gone to his head. He knows perfectly well it's illegal.'

'Sorry, Mary, I just couldn't resist winding you up a bit. But you know, it's because I can see the Rock from our windows at home, I can't help dreaming of climbing it.'

'Well, you had better stop dreaming. Sometimes people do get tempted, but it's not worth it, and you would lose your membership of our club if you did have a go.'

'Well I didn't know that! And, of course, I wouldn't want that.'

People were starting to drift back down and were

assembling near the minibus.

Alex and Ruth sat together on the way back, but somehow, surrounded by the chattering grown-ups, the magic slipped away. As the minibus approached a suburb on the outskirts of Edinburgh, where all the detached houses were hidden behind the bushes of extensive front gardens, Ruth got out onto the central aisle. She turned to Alex and queried:

'See you sometime soon?'

'Yes, sure, see you soon,' Alex replied.

As soon as she was off the bus he was kicking himself. Why hadn't he asked for her mobile number and given her his? What was the matter with him?

CHAPTER 3

A Strange Sense Of Compulsion

'Dad, you know you could go on Masterchef – that meal was unbelievable.' Alex savoured the last mouthful of chicken supreme.

'Aye, your dad's skills in the kitchen are way past mine now,' said Maureen.

'This house-husband thing is no so bad; I've loads of time to follow recipes and such like – no time for applying for jobs though.'

'Jock!' exclaimed Maureen.

'Only joking, Maureen,' Jock reassured her. 'As it happens, I've got an interview up at MacCreedy's to-morrow. Their warehouse man's on the sick and they need someone temporary – Jimmy Donaldson put me on to it.'

'Oh that sounds good, Jock,' said Maureen.

Alex yawned, pushed his chair back and muttered a few words about homework, to escape the conversation he'd heard so many times before about Jock getting 'a foot in the door' and turning a temporary job into a permanent one.

He sat down at his computer. Then he spotted something – beside his mouse was a strange brown bag. It was shaped like a pencil case, but smaller. He had never seen it before. He picked it up and turned it over. On one side there was what looked like a press-stud to open it. It wouldn't open.

'It's from them – those people from the future,' he whispered. 'Why have they put a bag on my computer desk?' He put it down to flick open his mobile as a text came in. On the screen was a message from Korin Katanya.

You are looking at a time/space travel bag. You will need it. Korin

It was five days since the most amazing day of his life – the day when he had achieved his first adult-level climb, when he had seriously fallen for a girl for the first time, and, as if those two things weren't enough for one day, when there had been the mind-blowing experience of contact with someone who claimed to be from the future.

It was, Alex thought, lucky that nothing much had happened at all in the intervening time because then he'd had time to think. When he wasn't thinking about the rock face and how his dad had nearly slipped and fallen, or about how adorable Ruth looked when she smiled, he was thinking about the oddly named outfit, STRAP.

Was it all some elaborate hoax? Impossible. Alex could believe that people could send weird messages. Even the expanding screen possibly could be explained: some new technology, perhaps, that had just been invented. But his dad being suspended on the stairs? No! That was the clincher. The contact was definitely from another civilisation. Did it matter if it was from somewhere else in the universe or, as Korin claimed, from the future?

He idled the evening away, surfing the internet for any clue about the acronyms STRAP and the other one that had been mentioned – SHARP. He found nothing. He went to bed early.

Half way through the night, he woke up. His mobile was going off with the strange ring tone that told him that the person on the other end would be Korin. As before, one of the buttons was glowing red. This time he pressed it voluntarily. The screen slid away and hovered several feet in front of him, filled with intense swirling colours that seemed to drift off the screen into the room. As before, it was as big as their television screen. Gradually the movement stopped and the following words appeared:

‹Welcome, Alex, to the STRAP organisation›

We would like to invite you to take part in STRAP Programme 10810. We are now going to send you our company policy. Please read it carefully.

There was a pause. Alex sat tense and excited on the edge of his bed, and then the following appeared on the screen:

‹Pre-Travel Information›

When we want you to undertake a journey to a different time, we will contact you on your mobile. You will know that it is a STRAP operator getting in touch because the ring tone is different to the one you normally use. We will only get in touch if we know that you can take on the travel mission. It is very important that no one sees you leave or return and that you do not TALK to anyone about your experiences. We will make sure by all the means we have at our disposal that your journey is undetected by family or friends.

‹Travel Information›

You will be gone from between one to two hours, your time. In the time to which you travel you may be away as long as two days, but no longer. Wearing clothes is not helpful, so you will need to strip down to your underpants. You will have received from us a small bag that you must wear. It doesn't need ties. It is called a time/space bag. When you have taken your clothes off, press the bag to your waist. It will attach itself to your skin without any discomfort, and it cannot be removed. The bag contains a small silver disc. When you arrive, press the disc to your forehead. The surface film will come away from the backing disc and dissolve harmlessly into your skin. This will relay pictures back to us recording everything you see. It only activates when it is worn, and it only lasts a short while, so do not put it on until AFTER you arrive in the past. Put the silver backing disc and your phone into the bag and secure the fastening.

‹Journey›

The project number for your journey is 10810 and you will be given instructions that tell you where you are going, what your name is and who you will meet. It identifies a Destination. Read these travel instructions very carefully, and when you are sure you have understood them, key in the project number 10810 and then press the **green button**. The system will be activated and you will be transported to the time indicated. Near to where you arrive there will be a pile of clothes suitable for the time and place. You must put these on as quickly as possible. You must then follow the instructions we have given above about the disc and your mobile.

The people you meet will mistake you for someone they know. It is hard to explain to you how this is possible, but to reassure you on this matter all you need to know is that when you put on the clothes mentioned above, you will also be putting on, without realizing it, the appearance of the person whose space you are entering. For some time travellers, it could be that the people they meet are not surprised that a stranger is amongst them. On your journeys you will find that you can help people; this you should do. Never do anything unkind.

‹Return Journey›
When it is time for you to return, you will feel the phone vibrating (not ringing). This is the message to tell you

that you must prepare to return to your own time. **You will not have long to respond to this**; whatever is happening you must get away as quickly as you can after the phone has started to vibrate. You will have to take off the clothes and leave them in a pile, preferably somewhere they cannot be seen too easily. Take the phone out of the bag, key in 10810 and press the **red button**.

‹After Your Visit›
We will contact you after your visit to give you an assessment of how well you have done.

Read these instructions several times. Korin Katanya will contact you in about ten minutes to give you the information you need for your current mission. In the unlikely event that you decide not to go, we will return your mobile to its original state…but we have every confidence, Alex, that you will not pass up this amazing opportunity.

Hmm, *they* might be confident, thought Alex, but I'm not! He was changing his mind all the time, one minute thinking it was the craziest and weirdest thing ever, the next being seriously tempted. Despite all efforts at using common sense, excitement was bubbling up inside him in a way that he had never felt before in his entire life. What was making him uncertain was that these STRAP people seemed to be issuing orders; they were like some kind of military outfit. But he did what they asked and read the instructions through several times. Then, when ten minutes had elapsed, Alex realized that his mobile was again no longer under his sole control. The screen cleared and Korin's face appeared. She smiled at him warmly and said:

'Hello Alex. I'm so glad you have decided to take up this travel option.'

'Hey, wait up there; I've not said any such thing.'

'But you are going to, aren't you, Alex? You couldn't miss the opportunity of a life-time – could you? Perhaps I should have contacted your friend Alistair instead. He lives very near by.'

'What? That idiot!'

'Here is your travel information and instructions, Alex. Take it or leave it, as you wish.'

She faded out and the screen filled with the following text:

‹Details of Current Travel Option›

‹Date›

April 1314.

‹Place›

Edinburgh.

‹Landing›

Near to a settlement.

‹Instructions›

After getting dressed, wait until someone comes out of one of the dwellings.

‹Destination›

Edinburgh Castle Rock.

‹Identity›

Known to everyone in the vicinity as Malcolm.

‹Conditions›

Weather benign – poverty as appropriate to these early times – Severe local unrest due to occupation of Scotland by English soldiers and subjection of the Scots in this area into service to the English against their will.

‹Equipment›
Mobile phone, travel bag.

You must get undressed down to underpants, press the time/space travel bag to your middle firmly and key in the code 10810.

I hope that you have read the previous instructions, but I will repeat the important elements.

When you arrive, take out the silver disc and press it to you forehead. The film backing will dissolve painlessly and harmlessly into your skin. The disc will relay pictures back to us. Remember to put the silver backing disc into the bag and put your mobile in the bag before looking round for the clothes that you will need to put on as quickly as possible.

As Alex read the instructions, he felt a strange sense of compulsion – of being hypnotised. As if in a trance, he took off his pyjamas and put on a pair of underpants. He pressed the time/space bag to his middle and keyed in the number 10810. As soon as he pressed the green button, he heard a high-pitched whine coming nearer and nearer until it seemed to be crashing into his ear drums. Then...Nothing.

CHAPTER 4

A Medieval Breakfast

The first feeling that came to him was one of cold, numbing cold! He was lying on his back, and for a while fear seemed to paralyse him. Then he sat up, spreading his hands out on...what? Something smooth and silky-soft. Just before panic took hold, he recognised both the touch and smell. It was moss, green and luxurious. He looked up. Of course! Yes...stars! Billions of them came into focus. He'd landed at night! No wonder he was cold. And he had no clothes on bar a pair of underpants!

His eyes were slowly adjusting to the light from the stars. He could just make out the bulge above his waist. He gave it a wiggle. It did not budge a millimetre. It was almost like part of his body. The instructions hammered in his head. He slipped out the silver disc and pressed it to his forehead. A thin film attached itself to his skin and then, just as STRAP had explained, the film seemed to disappear. He put the silver backing disc into the bag with his mobile and snapped the bag shut.

He stood up and looked about him.

'How am I supposed to find my medieval (or whatever) clothes in this darkness?' he mumbled. He felt a surge of anger at Korin, who had made it all seem so simple. It was cold and dark, and he couldn't help feeling he had not been given enough time to think about what he was about to do. If they had sent him back to 1314, what on earth was life like then? A terrible thought crept into his mind – would he ever get back to his own time? He thrust the thought away.

Suddenly he could see more clearly. In the far distance, the first pale rays of the rising sun were spreading out in the east. He swiveled a quarter turn to the north. And, yes – that must be the estuary. He could just make out the Firth of Forth glimmering in the early morning sun. He turned again to the west. In the distance there was a dense, black something or other – maybe a wood, a forest even. Beyond that, barely a kilometre away, lay the stark, forbidding face of the Edinburgh Castle Rock. Behind him were huts, black in outline under the shimmering panoply of stars. Yes. He was standing on the edge of some kind of settlement.

He scanned around in the dim light and saw a heap of... stones? No! OMG, were these the clothes he was supposed to wear? A rough knee-length hessian smock-thingee was the first thing he picked up; next a thinner vest-type garment with no sleeves; then some matching medieval…jeans? No! Not jeans…a jacket. But once dressed he was a whole lot warmer. The rough leather, hessian-padded footgear with metal tack bits on the soles looked dreadful. But he stomped up and down in them and realised that they gave him a good grip on the ground. For a moment, slightly hysterical laughter bubbled up inside him at the thought of what Ruth would say if she could see him dressed like this.

Signs of life were beginning to come from the dingy, mud-coloured homes: a small flickering light, the sound of a metal pan banging down on a hard surface, the scraping of a door opening. Curiosity drew him towards the largest of the black outlines. But before he could rekkie, he drew back as a figure emerged from the largest dwelling. It was a boy of about Alex's own age.

'Hello, is that you Malcolm? Come over from Caddick?' called the boy. 'The elders said you'd be coming over to join us.'

'Aye that's me,' called back Alex, not knowing what else to say.

'You've made it in good time. You must have set off a good hour ago,' the boy said.

Before Alex could reply, the sound of a horse's hooves made them both turn towards the sound. Someone was galloping directly towards them. As the rider got closer, Alex could make out the figure of a man. His long hair and a wide cloak streamed out in the wind behind him. As he drew nearer, Alex could see that the man was wearing a tunic studded with some kind of emblem. The horseman reigned in with a flourish and, as he did so, the other boy ran to meet him, bowing low.

'Welcome, Sire! My father, as you know, is forced to be at the castle but mother is awaiting your arrival.'

As the rider swung off his horse, Alex found rough reins being tossed towards him. He grasped them tightly and stood by the horse's head. The horse, panting hard from its exertions, butted him slightly and snorted warm breath on his neck.

'Well met, Ian,' said the man. He had a deep, commanding voice; Alex could tell in just those few words that he was someone used to being obeyed. 'And who may this be?' The rider nodded towards Alex.

'Sire, this is Malcom, come over from the farms at

Caddick. His family, though simple folk, are all true to your cause. Malcolm has been climbing with me and my father when father's not away at the castle, forced to be a servant to the Sassenachs.' The boy spat the last word out without concealing his hatred.

'I am glad to hear it. Well, Ian, take me directly to your mistress. We have much to discuss before the rest of your folk awake. It is already six of the morn.'

The young boy led the man towards the doorway of the biggest dwelling. Before he went in, the man turned round and called to Alex:

'My horse will need water, Malcolm.'

Alex was startled, for a moment, by being called a name not his own. But managed to call back: 'Aye, Sire,' repeating the form of address that the boy Ian had used.

A woman stepped out of the door smiling a welcome. That's got to be Ian's mother, thought Alex. He watched her drop a slight curtsey to the important visitor.

'Well met, Anne.' The man acknowledged the courtesy, and then all three disappeared into the house.

'Now what am I supposed to do?' Alex asked the horse. 'Maybe there's a water trough somewhere.

Come on.'

He led the horse towards the cluster of smaller buildings, and soon realised that there was a rough pathway leading into the middle of the dwellings. A few minutes later he came upon an enclosure where two other horses were quietly cropping the grass, and beside it was a long, low water trough. While the horse was drinking thirstily the other boy came running down the pathway.

'The Earl says to bring his saddle and bridle in, Malcolm. I'll give you a hand.'

Alex struggled to open the rickety gate of the enclosure, and so the boy took the horse's reins from him and led it into the small field, while Alex closed the gate. Nervously, Alex started unbuckling the saddle, something he had never done before in his life. The animal did a little skip to the side as if playing with him.

'Och…Malcolm are you still half asleep? I've never seen anyone make such a job of taking a saddle off a horse.' The boy whom Alex now knew as Ian gave him a friendly shove.

'I dearly wish I was still in bed,' Alex said, as if to explain his slowness.

'I can't believe it! How can you be sleepy when you've been chosen for such an honour, to be included on this most secret, most daring, most incredible plot! My mother says our names will go down in history – and you say you wish you were still in bed! I knew I should have put Alistair's name forward to my father.'

'What? Alistair – that dope!' Alex, who had made almost the same comment to Korin just a short while before, was amused to be slagging off a medieval Alistair.

'Mmm – you're right: he is a dope. But now you're acting just as dopey.'

Alex pulled the heavy saddle off the horse's back, while, with a quick flick of the wrist, Ian took the bridle off.

'Do you think you can wake up enough to carry the saddle up to the house?' the boy asked.

'Of course I can. I'm wide awake now.'

'Right– oh,' said Ian, pulling the enclosure gate shut behind them. 'Race you back, then.' He set off running, which was quite unfair as he only had the bridle to carry while Alex struggled with the heavier saddle. Ian disappeared round a corner, and Alex worried he wouldn't remember which dwelling he was supposed to go in. But he needn't have done because Ian was waiting at the doorway for him.

'Slow as a Sassenach,' he teased, pushing Alex

into the dark interior of the dwelling.

'Cheat,' Alex whispered back.

The first thing Alex noticed when he was inside was the smoke stinging his eyes. He stood blinking back unwanted tears as he tried to make out the scene in front of him. A fire with two metal pots suspended above it was in the middle of the room. Some of the smoke drifted upwards to a gap in the roof; the rest hung in the air.

Two women, one of them the woman who had greeted the rider, were busy stirring the cooking pots. Softly burning tapers attached to the walls provided the dim light. Alex could only just see across the room where about ten men were sitting round a large table.

The man who had arrived on horseback was sitting at the head of the table. He looked very much in charge. Dressed more grandly than the other men, he had an air of authority.

The women approached the table with the two pots of food.

'Sire,' one of them said, giving a small bob, 'There's hot broth and porridge a-ready for you.'

'I give ye thanks, Mistress Anne.' The man stood up, firm and strong, dominating the table. 'And thanks to our Lord for blessing this mission to free Scotland from the Sassenach yoke. Amen.'

All the men round the table repeated the 'Amen.'

'May our God in Heaven be with you Lord Thomas Randolph, Earl of Moray,' said one of the men.

'Amen,' murmured the others again.

At the name of Thomas Randolph, Earl of Moray, Alex felt as if his brain had received an electric shock – it was the name that he had been told about in all those boring primary school lessons! And from Zac on the bus only the other day! His mouth must have dropped open like an idiot's.

He felt Ian give him a gentle push forward.

'There's two places at the table for us, Malcolm. Did I not tell you what an honour has come to you?'

Alex and Ian squeezed themselves on to the rough wooden bench at the bottom of the table. Next to Alex was a small man with a bright-red, bushy beard who started eating with gusto. Alex poked at the mess on his plate cautiously. When he took a mouthful, though, he was amazed to find himself liking the mix of mushy porridge and meat. The coarse drink definitely contained something alcoholic, but he didn't know what.

After the meal, the women and old men went out with baskets and some sort of cutting or digging implements. They were no sooner gone than more burly, bearded men started to crowd through the door. They sat down on the mats on the floor. They numbered thirty in all, many with large canvas grips which turned out to hold a mixture of weapons and body armour.

Alex and Ian sat together at the back. The noise as the men talked, guffawed or called to each other was deafening. Then Thomas Randolph got up to speak, and slowly the noise subsided until there was silence. Every man looked at their leader with respect as he began to outline his plans for taking the stronghold of Edinburgh Castle and killing the Sassenach soldiers while they slept.

'The success of our plan rests on those of you who are prepared to scale the Rock and, with the advantage of surprise, take out the soldiers in their sleeping quarters. The rest of us can then take on the soldiers on the battlements. Many times in the past we have tried and failed to carry our armour up the terrible rock face on which the castle stands, but these two local boys say that they have found a way – they've made it to the top and know every handhold and foothold. They can be your guides.

Suddenly Alex found that all the men had turned

to look at him and Ian. He didn't know why, but he felt a red-hot flush burn his cheeks. He could see that the boy sitting next to him felt equally uncomfortable. He was staring hard at the floor. The blood started pounding in Alex's head as the meaning of the words he had just heard became clear. He and Ian were supposed to know the way up the Rock!

OMG!– I really hope that is true for Ian. I've been once on a climb supposed to resemble the castle face, and that was in broad daylight following Zac! I'm way out of my depth here. Alex felt fear grip his insides. Dimly he realised that the earl was still talking.

'Ian's father, Hamish, has assured me that the boys can do it. I am correct, here, am I not, Malcolm and Ian?' The earl paused and looked directly at the two. 'Speak up, boys. If what I have been told about you is wrong – speak now.'

Alex looked across at Ian and realised that the expression on his face was one of sheer terror. Slowly Ian got to his feet to answer. Surely, he was going to say that the earl was mistaken? But he didn't – quite the reverse.

'Sire, you are not wrong in what you have been told. Malcolm and I will lead the way up the rocks to the castle, following the route we have climbed before, and we are prepared to fall to our deaths if we have misled you.

The earl nodded. 'Well said, young Ian.'

He went on to tell of his spies and supporters – one of whom was Ian's father – who worked as servants in the castle for the English overlords. The plan was that they would add a stupefying drug to the English soldiers' wine the very next night.

'Many will be deep in their worst dreams or nightmares before they face our steel. They will die without making their peace with their maker, and that is a just death for these invaders of our land.'

This new plan was received with much surprise, and men started murmuring to each other.

'Quiet please, men.' The earl waited a moment for his men to stop muttering before going on. 'Well may you be surprised at my words, but I have been plotting tonight's work for many a long day. Those ten of you who are picked to follow the lads up the rock face must carry just your dirks, and any archers take your lightest bows. Anything heavier and you will not make it to the top. If successful, the climbers' first task, as I said, will be to silence forever the drugged soldiers in their sleeping quarters. They number over a hundred: so all must be killed! We only total thirty, so there is no other way. If the climbers are unsuccessful, the whole plan must be aborted.'

Thomas Randolph paused only for a moment to ensure the attention of his listeners.

'But if successful, after the killing you will silently make your way to the main courtyard to be ready to help Hamish and Jason overpower the guards at the gate, if they have not been successful in this already. It is less likely that the gate guards or those on the battlements will have succumbed to the temptation to drink the mead. However, we will be more evenly matched in numbers by then. Hamish will let down the drawbridge as soon as he has secured the keys. We will be waiting in full battle armour outside, our horses tethered out of earshot. If we have to fight the guards on the battlements, it will be because the wind will have carried the sound of the drawbridge being lowered to their ears.'

Alex listened intently to everything the earl said. Part of his mind was horrified at what the man was saying – butchering men in their sleep – but in some strange way he was totally drawn in, just as if he knew what it was to be oppressed by the English overlords.

The earl went on at length about how the men would be rewarded if the plan was successful. When he finished talking, he called Ian and Alex to his side and told them to sit with him while he picked the men who would do the climb. The earl had asked for volunteers; every man volunteered. Alex realised that what was driving these men was their hatred of the English, not, in fact, the handsome rewards that the earl had promised them and their families after their dangerous and exceptional service to the rightful King of Scotland. In the end, the earl picked ten of the youngest, strongest-looking men to join Ian and Alex on the climb.

CHAPTER 5

A Friendship?

Alex had spent all the morning with Ian, helping the men get their weapons and armour ready, polishing and shining blades of various shapes and sizes. At first, they had joked and laughed together, but as the morning wore on, Ian became more and more subdued. He spoke only when he had to, and his face was a blank, shutting everyone, including Alex, out. Alex knew there was something Ian was not letting on about, and he had to find out what it was.

Now they were sitting by a riverbank with two simple fishing rods in their hands. Ian had already caught two fish while Alex tried to copy him as best as he could, but obviously the fish knew he was an impostor. He hadn't caught one.

'I hope your climbing is going to be better than your fishing, Malcolm,' said Ian, lightening up a little.

'I'm not worrying about my climbing,' Alex replied, and then paused for a moment to make sure Ian was paying full attention. 'No it's not my climbing – or the men's – that I'm worried about – it's yours.'

This made Ian look up quickly. Alex could see that he had struck home. Ian looked annoyed and guilty at the same time.

'There's something I haven't told you, Malcolm. I know I promised that we would always do that climb together, but I wanted to be the first – the first to conquer the Rock! So I did another climb a week ago, and went up quite a bit further than we got to, though I didn't make it to the top. At the last stretch it's a sheer face, and then the wall. I started back down and I was getting really tired, but I spotted a possible alternative route, just near that last overhang... only an arm's length to the west from where we'd got stuck... So I told my father we had got all the way up to the wall.'

Alex felt his anger rising... so that was it! No one had climbed to the top. Had it been pride – had it been fear? Whatever it was, Ian had lied when he had told the earl that he and Malcolm had made it to the top.

'Why didn't you speak up when the earl asked you?'

'How could I? I would've shown my father up as a liar. It's all right for you. Your family has little standing – no one expects anything of you. But my father is the head of our village. Even though he's been humbled by being forced into the service of the English,

57

he's still the richest man in the neighbourhood. Besides, Malcolm, I *nearly* made it to the top.'

'Nearly, nearly – that's not good enough, is it?' Alex's temper flared up at his companion. 'You may be prepared to fall to your death as you told them back there, but I'm not!'

Alex jumped up and stomped off down the path away from the settlement. He felt so angry at the way Ian seemed to accept the fate that was handed to him. He walked on for quite some time before his anger drifted away, as it always did. He sat down on a fallen tree and thought about getting the mobile out from the bag and making an emergency call to return to the 21st century. But somehow that seemed like giving up.

'Just think,' he said to the small field mouse that was scurrying in the undergrowth nearby, 'I could tell Ruth that I have climbed the Castle Rock! She won't believe me, but it would be true! Tonight I can do what no 21st-century person is allowed to do! Climb the Rock. He turned round and made his way back to where he had left Ian fishing. The fishing was abandoned. Ian was lying face down in despair on the grass.

'Hey, who's the sleepy one now?' Alex joked, knowing that Ian wasn't asleep.

The boy stirred and slowly sat up. To his surprise, Alex could see smudges of tears on the face of this boy who made such a show of being hard.

'You've come back.' Ian muttered in a sullen voice. It was obvious that without his friend's support, all his confidence drained away. He needed Malcolm.

'Why, where did you think I was going?'

'Back home.'

'What, and miss the chance of climbing the forbidden Rock?'

'Forbidden – what do you mean?'

'Take no notice of me, Ian, I just had a fancy that sometime in the distant future, climbing the Rock will not be allowed.' Alex couldn't resist the absurdity of it.

'Oh Malcolm – you and your 'insights' into the future. Your mother and your lovely sister, Kathryn, are just as bad – full of fanciful thoughts.'

'Well there's no harm in it, is there?'

'Not as long as you keep your imaginings to yourselves, and only tell friends such as me. Anyway, if you can predict what is going to happen, tell me: will we climb the Rock tonight or will we fall to our deaths?'

'Ah, now there's a question.' Of course, Alex knew part of the answer but not the whole. To encourage Ian he said: 'I'm sure we will succeed.' He did-n't add that his school history books did not record whether any of the climbers fell to their deaths. That was how history always was – only the doings of the rich and powerful were recorded. You learnt of the kings and lords in the medieval times, and of the politicians and presidents in modern times. No one re-membered the names of any ordinary people who died in battles.

'So who is going to lead the climb, then?' Ian asked.

'We'll lead together, you and I.' Alex saw disap-pointment flash across Ian's face and added: 'you in the front and me right behind you.'

Ian gripped his hand hard. 'Yes, yes, it is right that I should lead. Malcolm, you are a true friend. We will not fail.' The two stared at each other, hand held in hand. At that moment, something passed between them: a never-to-be-broken bond of friendship, though only Alex understood that, unbelievably, it would cross the barrier of time.

Now, with the mood changing to one of opti-mism and hope, the two of them sat back down on the riverbank and caught a couple more fish, both of them laughing as Alex hooked one out. As they walked back to the village with the basket of fish between them, a thought suddenly struck Alex.

'How come you called my sister 'lovely?' he grinned, wondering whether remarking about a girl would wind someone up in medieval times. It certainly did, because Ian went bright red.

'You know, I mean no disrespect.'

'Of course not, how could I think such a thing.' There was a silence and then Ian asked, glancing awkwardly at his friend, 'Is there no one you admire the way I do your Kathryn?'

'Oh yes, there is,' said Alex, thinking of Ruth.

CHAPTER 6

The Night Of The Killing

'Wake…Wake up!' a harsh voice startled Alex awake. He, Ian and the others who were to take part in the assault had been asleep for a few hours to replenish their strength. They had all fallen asleep on rush mats on the floor of the main dwelling.

Candles cast a wavering light across the room. Alex could see that the women were moving about with bowls of cold water and a jug. The men would either fill the jug and pour it over their heads or scoop it into their cupped hands to splash over their faces. Alex and Ian copied them, gasping with the shock of it but now totally awake and alert.

Thomas Randolph, Earl of Moray gave the command for those climbing the Rock to leave the village. Each climber had a metal flask to hook onto their belts or pockets. They had only the starlight to guide them. They stole through the homestead quietly, scarcely making a sound; then through the woods until they reached the sheer, black face of the Rock. Still under cover of trees, the little group shook hands with each other in turn; each hand clasp conveying the person's good wishes for the other's safety.

The climb began. Ian, calm and confident, led, with Alex close behind him, and the men spread out one-by-one but with only an arm's span or so between them. At first, it seemed easy. There were plenty of handholds and ledges on which to place feet securely. The human chain zig-zagged its way slowly but surely up the dark rock. A third of the way up, the rake of the cliff sharpened and the ledges became narrower and narrower. Alex's heart started to thud painfully. He broke out in a sweat, which rapidly chilled on his forehead and trickled down his neck. He was, he realised, for the first time in his life, really afraid – afraid he'd miss a handhold and go crashing down the side of the mighty volcanic rock to a messy death.

'Stop now for a moment, if you can.' Ian's voice floated quietly downwards on the night air.

Alex was on the smallest of ledges but he paused for a moment. He shook first one hand and then the other to try to release the muscles that ached with the intensity of gripping.

'I'm going on now.' Ian's voice came again.

Alex started climbing again, watching Ian's moves and repeating them. The man behind him did the same and the man behind him also; they didn't have ropes, but they might as well have, so synchronized were their movements. The light from the stars was amazingly bright – much brighter than in any 21st-century town or city. Even without a full moon they could still see where to go.

Whenever a thought came into his head, Alex thrust it out, concentrating, concentrating, remembering the moves, how to gain benefit from even the smallest crack or crevice. As they toiled in silent unison, guided by desperate mental concentration, the rock seemed to get ever smoother and the zig-zags became shorter and sharper. Alex realized that, at this point, there was no going back; there were only two options; reach the top or fall!

'Malcolm,' Ian called. 'This is as far as I got last time on my own. We now track to the left – then it's upward again. If I drop off you must continue.'

'Then don't, matey. Dropping off is strictly out of order, and that's a command!'

A muffled guffaw echoed eerily downward.

Ian leaned away to the left, stretching his arm up and out as far as he could, just managing to grip on to the smallest of jutting rock to lever himself up another length. Alex followed his action exactly and found that his feet were now on a small ledge. The man behind did the same.

Then a low swinging light appeared above them, and two swarthy figures were silhouetted briefly against the night sky. They had negotiated the overhang! They were almost at the wall of the castle! A proper wooden ladder was lying downwards over the last two or three metres. With the energy which motivates the near desperate in sight of the destination, they each took hold in turn of the bottom rung and moved cautiously upward until two sets of strong hands lifted them over the low parapet wall.

They both collapsed on the ground, exhausted, and watched from a horizontal position as the powerful outline of the two men helped the weary climbers, one by one, over the last obstacle. Every man made it. Not a single soul lost!

All the men crowded round the two boys, pulling them up on to their feet, clapping them on the shoulder, muttering quiet praise and toasting them with an amazingly revitalising concoction in their flasks. It poured down their aching throats into their bellies, warming them up from within, recharging them with energy. Alex felt a surge of exhilaration as he realized what he had done – he wanted to rush around whooping like a Premier League footballer who had just scored!

One of the two burly men who had helped them over the wall was Ian's father, Hamish. Now his arm went around his son and he clasped the boy to him. In the low hushed whisper that they were all using, in case there were English solders who had not succumbed to the drugged liquor, he said: 'I'm so proud of you, son.' Then he shook Alex's hand. 'And you too, Malcolm.'

After only a few minutes, though, once they had recovered from the strenuous climb, the men were silently organizing themselves ready for the next part of the plan. Hamish was to lead a small number of men to the gatehouse where they might possibly find the sentry guards still awake. They would need to use the element of surprise to overcome these men, if that was the case.

Most of the group was to go to the sleeping quarters of the garrison and carry out the killing of the English soldiers now lying in a drugged stupor, just as the earl had outlined earlier in the day.

Alex realized that he and Ian were supposed to accompanying these men. A man called Jason who was in command at this point whispered to them that they should come with him. To Alex's dismay, it seemed that the earl had considered that they would be in less danger with the greater number of men, and he also wanted them to bear witness for future generations to how the Scots had overcome their Sassenach oppressors.

The thought of what he was about to see made Alex feel physically sick. As the men started to run towards the dormitory building, keeping to the shadows as far as possible, Alex wondered if he could slip away unnoticed; only the fear of being found by an English soldier and stabbed to death on sight, kept Alex running beside Ian.

The barracks loomed ahead, lit by the flicker of a wall torch. At the door, a soldier sprawled out on his back, was the only obstruction to the entrance. A large drinking cup was clutched in his fist; it looked as if he had tumbled off the stool nearby.

Jason bent down and, without hesitation, drew the sharp blade of his dagger right across the man's throat. Blood spurted up. Alex stared at it mesmerized as it quickly formed a pool, glistening in the moonlight. The eyes of the man that had been closed a moment earlier, flicked open and stared unseeingly as the person who had killed him stepped across his body.

Ian pushed Alex roughly forward into the barracks and said:

'We have been commanded to bear witness, Malcolm. Follow Jason. Remember these are the enemies who have taken our freedom from us.'

'I know, I know Ian, but I just can't watch.'

But watch he did, as if transfixed. About fifty men lay sleeping in that huge barracks, and the figures of the men who had climbed the cliff face behind him moved swiftly from one to the other, bending over a body almost as if caring for it, only to raise a sharp blade to thrust it deep, or to slash a mortal wound. At first could be heard only the uneven sound of men sleeping, the rumble of snores... then came gurgling sounds, and deep groans... a low gurgle, sigh, groan, these sounds went on... and on... until not one Sassenach soldier was left alive.

To Alex's horrified eyes, the men who had so recently seemed friendly, likeable chaps had turned into killing machines. As he stood in that awful place, he thought about STRAP's invisible camera on his forehead and he knew that, for some reason that he did not understand, they wanted to see this event.

How long it all took, Alex couldn't say, but when he and Ian finally followed Jason and the men back down the slope towards the gatehouse, he couldn't speak and he desperately wanted to run – he didn't know where to, just to run.

At the gatehouse, Hamish and his men had engaged in a short but swift skirmish with four men who were, unlike those in the barracks, not asleep. However, they'd been easily overcome, not suspecting anything was wrong when they saw Hamish enter the guardroom. Their bodies lay in an untidy heap, their weapons still in their hands.

Hamish had let the drawbridge down. Thomas Randolph and three knights in full armour accompanied by about thirty foot soldiers moved into the castle grounds. This was the first that the now much-depleted English forces knew of the trouble they were in.

Alex, standing near the gate, heard a cry come from the top battlements:

'Enemy within, Enemy within!'

Then Thomas Randolph shouted his orders to his men to cover the stairs. The English up on the battlements had no idea that most of their forces had already been killed, and so, instead of staying in the relative safety up on the battlements, they came rushing down the stairwells.

At first, Alex watched in a daze as the men attacked each other in a frenzy, most wielding swords or the razor sharp Scottish dirks. One huge English soldier lay about him with an axe, until a knife was thrown into his back and he fell to his knees and then with a thud to the ground. At this point, Alex walked away, no longer able to watch. But it was soon over; the English were outnumbered and quickly overcome. The Scots had lost a few men and Jason was sitting on the ground unable to walk because of a wound in his left leg.

'Come, Malcolm,' Ian said, 'help Jason to his feet.'

They went over to where Jason was struggling to get up. Alex could see blood pouring from a gash in his leg. Mindless of the cold, he quickly took off the upper garment he was wearing, used a knife to cut it into strips and tied the strips tightly round Jason's leg to stop the blood.

'Well thank you, lad,' Jason said, holding out a hand for them to pull him up.

A quiet had fallen on the scene of mayhem, with all the men unsure of what to do next. Then Thomas Randolph silently led the way to the entrance and all followed him. The earl got up onto a low wall to address the men as they gathered round. They all looked tired, weary, as if all their energy had been drained from them; it wasn't only Alex that was feeling the strain of the horror. Now the heat of battle was over, the men were feeling it too. But Thomas Randolph was a real leader; he knew he must rally their spirits.

'Listen to me, men,' he said in a loud commanding voice. 'This is your moment of great glory, which will be remembered by your descendants for centuries to come! You can be proud that you have been here this night. We have won a great victory! It is only the start, though, and much more lies before us, but this day be full-hearted. We have won back what is ours: the Castle of Edinburgh is once again in the hands of the Scots!'

The cheering was loud and long. Men held up their fists and pumped the air in victory salute: just, thought Alex, like the winners of a football match!

The earl spoke some more and Alex's attention wandered, but then he heard:

'Here on this 14th day of March 1314, I proclaim you, Ian and you, Malcolm, to be, from this day on, squires to a nobleman. You will be welcome in the household of my cousin, the Earl of Carrick, younger brother to our new King of Scotland, Robert the Bruce. You will have a future worthy of your bravery tonight.'

He paused and the men cheered, slapping Ian and Alex on the back.

'More glory lies before all of us...and more battles. Now we must go and let those in the villages know of our victory.'

There was more cheering. Some had started to take drinks from their flasks. Alex could see that Ian was talking with his father, Hamish. Men were beginning to tell each other what they had done. He edged to the back of the group and without a backward glance quickly made his way down the hill away from the castle. The phone was vibrating in the time/space travel bag. He passed excited groups of settlers hurrying up to the castle with hay carts, loaded with food and flagons of mead - to join in the celebration.

The phone continued vibrating in the time/space travel bag. He reached a small clump of trees, quickly found a hiding place, took off the clothes and left them in a pile. Then he snapped open the bag, took out the phone and keyed in 10810. From far away he heard a high-pitched whine. It came nearer and nearer until it was banging in his head. Then...Nothing.

CHAPTER 7

Two Unexpected Meetings

'Alex, you've been weird lately, I mean really weird.' Alistair had his foot poised on the seat of the park bench. He gave Alex a questioning look before stepping onto the seat then up on to the top of the bench, balancing there in mock-gymnastic stance and then toppling onto the grass behind. Alex lifted his eyes slightly to watch his friend's performance. He was sitting, his head cupped in his hands, elbows resting on his knees looking miserable.

'Maybe it's being with you that's done it,' replied Alex. 'Weirdness must be catching. I'm all psyched up for you to do one of those double back-flip things and a dance around the fountain right now, with orchestral accompaniment.' His voice was full of sarcasm.

'At least I don't go for days without saying anything more than 'uhhh?' whenever I'm asked something, or even if I'm not asked anything, which is what you've been doing for the last couple of weeks – as if the whole universe was a total mystery to you.'

'Alistair, you've got it right just there: the universe is a total mystery to me.' Alex knew that Alistair was joking, but *he* wasn't. He was forcing back thoughts of bodies with knives being thrust into them, of men sleeping one moment and dead the next, dreadful sounds and worse smells. He felt about a hundred years old. He wished for the umpteenth time he could tell his friend what had happened to him.

It was nearly two weeks since he had come back from the 14th century, and he was finding it difficult to adjust. His mum had noticed, of course, and put it down to him working too hard for the end-of-year tests, or perhaps, she had wondered, had he fallen for a girl? She was almost right there: but not quite in the way she imagined. Thoughts of Ruth and their shared success on the climb were the only things that elbowed out the dark memories.

Alex caught sight of Mike and Donald, the guys he and Alistair had arranged to meet at the fountain at the west end of Princess Street Gardens. They were slouching along with their hoods up. Despite them being almost ten minutes late they showed absolutely no signs of hurrying.

'So good of you to get here on time,' said Alistair witheringly. 'I've been stuck here for ages with Mr. Fun-a-minute-not-Alex-McLean.'

Donald consulted his watch, his floppy blond hair obscuring almost all of his face as he looked down at his wrist.

'Oooh, ten minutes late, mate – such a crime!'

Alistair pulled a face.

'Now you come to mention it, Alex has been a pain just lately. He didn't even turn up for cricket practice on Thursday,' said Mike, turning to look at Alex. 'What's with you, mate? Has some girl given you the thumbs down? Is it that girl you go climbing with?'

'No, it's not! And will you all just shut up.' Alex felt his temper rising. He clenched his fists, and suddenly the others were aware that there was something going on that was more than they bargained for. Quick glances were exchanged that gave the same message – cool it.

Alex calmed down. He knew he was seriously over-reacting: 'I've just had a bit of hard time lately,' he added. 'I mean, if you'd rather I left, that's fine by me.' He glared round at his friends.

'Don't be daft, mate. We're only messing.' Alistair held his hands up in mock surrender. 'What's everyone say we head on up Princes Street and see what's about talent-wise.'

'Good idea,' said Mike.

'I'm starving,' said Donald.

There was a chorus of: 'what's new?' from the others and the joking now turned on Donald who, being a little on the tubby side, was quite used to teasing about his liking for food.

They strolled out of The Gardens and up into the busy city.

They were soon engulfed by the busy throng of people on Princes Street, a magnificent thoroughfare that could claim to be one of Europe's most elegant streets. Although not nearly as grand as in times gone by, tourists from all over the world still came to stroll along its length, with shops on one side and the view of the castle and The Gardens on the other.

There were so many shoppers and tourists it was impossible for the lads to stay four-abreast. Donald and Alistair went in front, larking about as ever, especially when they passed one of the many tartan tat shops. One or other of them would do a little highland jig and expect applause or at least a laugh from the two following. Mike, thinking Alex was having girl problems, had taken it upon himself to tell Alex how he was making out, or rather (it seemed) not making out, with a girl called Shelly who had 'the most amazing legs – up to her armpits'. Shelly, it transpired, was a friend of Mike's sister, Anna, who had said that she and her friends were going to be in Starbucks that afternoon. So it was no surprise that the four of them were shortly to be found seated at a Starbucks table with a bottle of coke in front of each of them.

So far no sign of Anna or the 'legs up to the armpits' Shelly.

But a girl did appear behind Alex. She grinned over his shoulder at the others, put her finger to her lips to shush them, and then covered Alex's eyes with her hands.

'Guess who!!!' Alex's mates bellowed out, drowning out Ruth's quieter voice saying the same words. After a few random guesses at names – all male – Alex decided to feel the hands. He knew at once:

'Ruth!' Alex whipped round trying, and failing, not to look pleased. 'Hey – It's great to see you. Guys, this is the girl I've been telling you about, the one who's such a good climber. Come and join us, Ruth, I'll get you a drink. What would you like? A coke?'

'A coke would be great.'

Alistair stood and gave up his seat for her, looking round for a spare chair. Just then his mobile buzzed. Everyone waited while he took the call, which was obviously from his sister Anna. Alistair slipped the phone back in his pocket:

'Anna and her mates are up at Burger King on George Street. I'm away up there. What about you guys?'

'Oh, yes, yes, we're with you there,' said Donald and Mike, both obviously keen to leave Alex and Ruth on their own.

'Tell you what, though, Ruth,' Donald turned to say before leaving, 'we're all dead impressed by your superior rock climbing skills. Alex gives you a great write up.'

Ruth looked pleased, and Alex felt distinctly sheepish as she flopped into a chair beside him.

'I was going to phone you…' Ruth started. 'The club contacted me this morning to see if I wanted to go on an outdoor climb, a two-day trip in the August holidays. I said I would. Are you going? They said they were going to email you this morning. Did they?'

'I didn't open up my computer this morning so I don't know. But I'd love to go. Where is it?'

'Perthshire somewhere. We can get a lift there at dawn. The route is via the bridge, with Zac and five others, then the climb, then a sleep-over in a croft: they don't ask for a fixed fee, just a donation.'

'Wow, fantastic! I'm sure there's no reason I can't come. I'll check my emails as soon as I get back.'

'It will be so much more fun with you coming,' Ruth said.

'Hey, I haven't got that drink for you yet.' Alex pushed his chair back to get up; then a thought struck him:

'Were you waiting for someone?' he asked.

'Yes, I was supposed to be meeting my friend Meg and her mum. I was at that table over there when I spotted you.' Ruth nodded towards a small table by the wide window from where there was an amazing view of the castle. 'They're about fifteen minutes late. It's not like them. '

'Well it's lucky for me, they've not turned up. It means we can spend some time together. I'll go and get you that drink.'

When they emerged from Starbucks, they wondered aimlessly, looking in shops, and then decided to walk in the castle gardens.

'I love the Ross Fountain. Can we walk that way?' asked Ruth.

'Of course,' Alex replied. 'I met up with the guys there earlier this afternoon. What is it you like about it?'

'I think it's beautiful. I love all that old-fashioned kind of stuff. When I was really little, I used to come here with my mum. I used to make up stories about water-fairies that lived in the fountain and came awake at night. They would fly to my bedroom – I really, really believed I went flying with them. I would tell my mum and she would say I'd been dreaming, of course.'

Alex grinned. 'You – a fairy – sparkly wings and wand!' He stood up on his toes and pirouetted round clumsily, hands above his head.

'Oh shut up! I wish I hadn't told you. I've never told anyone that before.'

Alex stopped in his tracks. 'Sorry,' he said, no longer laughing 'that was well out of order.' Nothing was said then for a bit and Alex worried that he had blown it.

They reached the same bench where he'd been with his mates earlier that afternoon and sat down. Alex looked across at the Rock, and as always had a momentary flashback to the night of the climb. His face darkened.

'If you believed in fairies when you were little, perhaps you could believe in stranger things than that now.'

'What do you mean?'

'I mean that some very, very strange things have happened to me just lately.'

'Like what?'

'Like, I've climbed the Castle Rock... I've climbed it.'

'You've what? After all that Mary said about it being illegal!' Ruth stared at the vast bulk of granite in front of her. 'When? I don't believe you – tell me you're teasing me!'

'I'm not teasing. I have climbed the Rock and it wasn't illegal.'

'What do you mean – wasn't illegal?'

Just then a girl – an extremely attractive girl – with black, curly hair, wearing an expensive-looking tracksuit, jogged towards them. She almost passed them, but then turned and flopped down on the bench beside Ruth.

'Hi, Alex,' she said.

'Korin?' Alex was stunned… 'What are you doing here?'

'Aren't you going to introduce me to your friend Ruth?'

'Doesn't sound as if you need an introduction.'

'I don't know you,' said Ruth, staring at the beautiful girl beside her. 'How do you know my name?'

Korin didn't answer.

Alex leant forward: 'Ruth, this is Korin. I know her because…because she contacted me a while back.' He searched desperately for the right words. A few moments previously he had been on the point of telling Ruth about his mind-blowing experiences, but now all he could think was that Ruth would be imagining that this stunning girl was somehow interested in him.

'Korin is… she's not of this world. I mean she's as much out of it as your fairies.'

'Oh thanks, Alex. I've never been compared to a

fairy before – although our scientists can devise a few of those if they want to.'

Ruth was looking first at Alex and then at Korin with a total look of disbelief on her face.

'I'm sorry, Ruth, it must all seem a bit strange to you,' Korin stood up facing them both. 'But I really wanted to meet you, so I just popped by to say hello. Alex can explain all about me when I've gone, and I can't stay long. You see, I come from a time way, way in the future. Trips like the one I'm doing now aren't really allowed, but we knew Alex was going to tell someone and we sort of worked out it would be you.' Korin sat down again, this time next to Alex.

'Why did you think I would tell someone?' Alex was indignant.

'Well, time travel in itself is stressful, but what you went through back there was more than that, it was harrowing. The medical lot at STRAP said you could suffer real trauma and not be able to time travel again if you didn't have someone you trusted to talk to about it; apparently that relieves stress.

'I have been feeling awful – I mean really awful; suicidal, I think.'

'Exactly. The trouble is there is no way anyone from the 21st century would believe you when you said you had gone back in time to 1314. Like Ruth's mother, when she told her about flying with the fairies, they would say you've been dreaming, wouldn't they? And at your age it would be seen as some sort of psychological disorder. They would cart you off to hospital.

'Well, of course, I knew I couldn't tell my mum. But I thought maybe Ruth would believe me.'

Korin leaned across Alex and said to Ruth:

'Ruth, do you believe Alex has travelled back in time and that I come from a time in the future?'

Ruth shook her head slowly. 'I think you are both playing some stupid, wretched trick on me and I think it's really nasty of you. Alex, I just can't believe I have been so wrong about you!' She stood up, looking as if she was near to tears. She was about to storm off, but Alex jumped up and grabbed hold of her wrist.

'Don't go, Ruth, please don't go. Plea…se listen to us.'

'I think I've heard enough of your ridiculous lies!' Ruth was glaring angrily at Alex, but she hadn't walked off.

'Ruth, where's your phone?' Korin's voice cut into the silent anger.

'What?' Ruth stared at Korin, who was still sitting

calmly on the bench.

'Where's your phone?' Korin repeated.

Ruth felt in her pocket. It obviously wasn't there. 'Why are you asking me that?'

'Because I know you haven't got it, and I know as well that it is behind the counter in Starbucks, and that when you go to get it, they will give it to you, and there will be extra buttons on it like the ones on Alex's phone. It will convince you that we are speaking the truth. Please sit down, Ruth, and we will try to explain things in a better way to you.'

Ruth sat down again, almost as if in a trance. She was still searching in her pockets, but she didn't have her phone.

'My phone's gone – I never lose it.'

'We took it out of your pocket in Starbucks – we can become invisible when we want to.'

'Ruth, I'm so sorry about this. I…' Alex was pleading with her '…I didn't want you to get involved, not like this. I can so totally understand you thinking this is some kind of a hoax, but believe me, it isn't.' His words sounded sincere to Ruth, but still the whole thing seemed fantastical. She stared at the Rock as if it would provide an answer.

'Is that why you said you had climbed the Rock?'

she asked quietly.

'Yes. They – that's Korin's outfit; they're called STRAP – they sent me back in time to 1314. I became one of the Scottish rebels who climbed the Rock to overcome the sleeping English. I saw the killing…I saw our history.'

'Oh my God, Alex.' Ruth spoke quietly but something about her voice told Alex that she was beginning to believe him.

'I'm going now,' said Korin, 'but here is one thing to help you believe what Alex says. Nearly everyone from our time has seven digits, not five on their hands.' Korin put her hand on Ruth's knee and Ruth looked down at it. She slowly counted the fingers. On Korin's beautiful, perfectly shaped hand, there were six fingers and a thumb.

'You know' said Korin, 'Alex is not the only boy from the 21st century to travel back in time. The first was a boy called Danny Higgins. He has set up a blog page called 'dannydoestimetravel' – you can find it on the internet – that might help to convince you.'

Korin started to walk away. Alex jumped up to follow her.

'Korin, no one has got back to me after 1314. I mean you said there would be an assessment.'

'You'll find it on your computer when you get back, along with information about what's coming next.'

'Why have you changed Ruth's mobile? – she's not going to time travel for you, not Ruth.'

'No, she's not – stop worrying, Alex.'

Alex sat down beside Ruth and they watched Korin walk away. At some point they couldn't see her anymore, but they weren't sure if it was because she had turned a corner, disappeared among the other people strolling in the park, or simply vanished.

CHAPTER 8

Summer Holiday Cutbacks

After going back to Starbucks, retrieving Ruth's mobile and seeing her off on her bus, Alex walked home. When he got in, his mum wasn't back from work and his dad was out. He rushed upstairs and switched on his computer. A message from STRAP appeared on the screen.

‹Assessment Message to Alex McLean from STRAP – the Scientific Testing and Recording of Aggression Processes›

Hello, Alex. By the time you read this, you will have met with Korin in the park. We assess the people who undertake time-travelling for us under various headings, as you will see below. Your assessment is short, but shows good work on your part. Congratulations.

Aptitude for Time Travel› Good.
Memory› Good, though occasional lapses.
Physical Attributes› For someone from the 21st cen-

tury, good.

Bravery› Very good.

Understanding of the Customs of the Period Visited›Average but this is to be expected as no training and little advance warning was given; clearly the operative was not provided with a great deal of information from the education processes of the time..

‹**Information Re Next Assignment**›

You are in the middle of an important assignment. We cannot stress too much to you how useful your work has been, not just to us, but to the whole of humanity. We want you to carry on with your involvement in the events that followed the Edinburgh Castle massacre. Please find out as much as you can about this period of history from the records you have in your time.

We will contact you again soon.

As soon as Alex had finished reading, the message disappeared from his screen. He turned towards the window and stared out at his panoramic view of the castle and the city of Edinburgh. When he was younger he took it for granted, but now every time he looked out of the window, he could see himself on that dark, desperate night, scrambling up the Rock behind Ian. Now STRAP had said: 'we want you to carry on with your involvement in the events that followed…' Did that mean he would meet Ian again? For some reason that he would have been completely unable to explain, he desperately wanted to see again the boy he had shared so much with in 1314.

Of course, the other person he wanted to see again was Ruth, even though he had only said good-bye to her a few hours before. He thought of sending her a text to find out if she was OK, but then decided to phone. He selected her number and listened impatiently to the rings:

'Hi Alex,' Ruth answered quickly.

'Are you all right?'

'Yes, I'm fine, but I can't get it all out of my head. I read the STRAP page on my phone loads of times before it went.'

'It disappeared, did it?'

'Yes, I think after about the fifth read it just scrolled away.'

'They don't like leaving evidence around.'

'Alex, you're not going to go back in time again are you?'

'I don't know, Ruth. It's such an amazing experience. I can't really explain it, but I feel as if I am in the middle of some unfinished business. I don't think I can walk away from it now.'

'Do you trust these people?'

'No, not a hundred-per-cent, but I think it's in their interest to keep me alive.'

'OMG, Alex, that sounds so desperate, like you have been sucked into a spy ring or something.'

'Ruth – I can't tell you what it means to be able to talk about it to someone.' There was silence on the other end of the phone for a moment.

'That's OK, Alex.'

'I never really explained to you about the friend I made. His name was Ian and we climbed the Rock together. I just have this feeling that I have to go back for him. I don't know what it is, but there is something I must do.'

'If you feel like that, then you do have to do it. You sound just like my dad when he's trying to explain to mum why he's got to go and do some really dangerous climb.'

'Does your mum understand?'

'Yes, I think she does, but, of course she worries.'

'But you understand him, don't you?'

'Yes I do, but I still worry as well. Have you contacted the club yet about the Perthshire climb?'

'I'm on to it as soon as I stop talking to you.'

'Well, I'm saying goodbye to you then. But just make sure you're around when the trip is on, not stuck in some weird medieval century.'

'I'll be here, I promise,' said Alex. 'Bye, Ruth, and thanks a hundred times.'

Alex looked at his emails, found the message from Zac about the two-day climbing trip and sent a reply to say he wanted to go. Then he sat back and went over in his mind the message from STRAP. He needed to find out more about Scotland in the 14th century. He knew from his junior school history lessons that the Battle of Bannockburn followed just three months after the taking of Edinburgh Castle. He put Bannockburn into his search engine and found just how near the site of the battle was to Stirling Castle. His parents had never taken him there, which was strange, considering that they had often mentioned visiting the place before he was born. He had always supposed that it was at Stirling Castle where his dad had asked his mum to marry him.

He began trawling through different websites about Bannockburn. One thing in the story he found difficult to understand: why did the English King Edward come up into Scotland to meet with disaster at Bannockburn? It was easy enough to understand why Robert the Bruce wanted to chase the English out of Scotland and be king, but why did the English king march north? Then Alex came on the piece of information he was looking for: Stirling Castle, then occupied by the English, was being besieged by the Scots, but a truce was signed in 1313, agreeing to the lifting of the siege on the understanding that the castle would be given to the Scots if the English did not come to relieve it by Midsummer's day 1314. This was just three months after the Edinburgh massacre – that was why the English king marched north! He didn't want to lose that castle as well!

It would be useful to have names of the main players, he thought. He clicked on to the Stirling Castle official site – not much help really, full of information about restaurants and corporate entertainment. But it did tell him that the castle was built mainly during the 16th century; they called it a 'renaissance' castle. So it would now be very different to how it was in 1314.

Suddenly, a gentle tap on his door warned him that his mum was about to walk in to investigate his internet use. Maureen sailed in before a 'come in' was offered, confident that it was her duty to check that Alex wasn't on one of those dreaded chat-room sites.

'Hi, Mum,' Alex said 'I didn't know you were back from work.'

'I've been back over an hour Alex. What's been keeping you away from the kitchen? I thought you'd be down for a snack.'

Maureen peered quickly at the screen and gave a puzzled frown: the site on the screen showed a picture of Stirling Castle.

'Goodness! They've not given you a new history topic, have they? You're breaking up in a couple of weeks.' Alex shook his head, but didn't offer an explanation.

'Why have you and Dad never taken me on a trip to Stirling? You've talked about when you were there before I was born, but I've never been, and it's only forty miles away.'

'Do you know, Alex, I think you must be psychic. Your dad and I were just saying the other night we ought to go, but that's because we were talking about what to do over the summer.'

'Oh yeah?' Alex swung his chair round to face his mum, who had sat down on his bed.

'Well, it's like this Alex...' His mum was looking

worried, 'we know you'll be disappointed, but we don't think we ought to book a holiday this year.' Maureen scanned Alex's face anxiously for signs of him being upset.

The McLeans had been going to Spain for a week's holiday with Maureen's sister Barbara, her husband Steve and their two children every year since Alex was little. Normally Alex would have been disappointed about missing the break, but somehow now it didn't seem to matter at all.

'Don't worry, Mum, I understand completely. It's OK, really it is.'

After a lot more explanations about why she and Jock had made the momentous decision to scupper the family holiday, Maureen finally left, much relieved that she hadn't got a sulky son on her hands. Amazingly, Alex seemed happy to swap Spanish sunshine for coach trips to local places of interest.

Later that evening she and Jock decided that Alex's easy acceptance of no summer holiday wasn't just because they had an angel for a son, but more because he had got his mind on other things. They both agreed that it looked as if Maureen was right in her assumption that Alex's recent 'odd moods' had been brought on by him falling for a girl. Alex had come down to tell them how he had met up by chance with Ruth that afternoon, and that she had told him about the opportunity for a two-day climbing trek out into Perthshire organized by Zac and the club. Jock and Maureen had immediately given the trip their blessing and marked it on the family calendar – second week in August.

'Did you see how excited he was about sleeping in the croft on the climbing trip?' Maureen said.

'Oh definitely,' Jock winked. 'But you know, she's a lovely girl. Comes from a very good family.'

'It's the best thing we ever did, getting him interested in climbing, and that was all down to you, Jock.'

'Yes, but Alex is going to go way, way past me as a climber.'

'You don't mind, do you?' Maureen looked anxiously at her husband.

'Of course I don't mind, dafty…he's my son. He's going to make us really proud, Maureen. Aye, and he'll be a better climber than my brother, Martin.'

'Jock!' Maureen exclaimed.

'Well, you know how he brags.'

'Aye he does.'

'Now let's plan that trip to Stirling Castle. You know it brings back the best memories I've ever had.

And Alex is right, we should have taken him before now.'

CHAPTER 9

A Day Trip To Stirling Castle

Alex spent the next two weeks finding out more about Scottish history. He borrowed a book from the Library called: 'Bannockburn 1314: Battle for a Nation' by an author with the strange name of 'Tabraham'. It had detailed pictures of the battle and maps. From these he learned that no-one knew the battle's exact location. For some reason, Alex found himself puzzled by this: a place where hundreds, possibly thousands, had died in bloody combat and there was no trace of it!

A week into Alex's school holidays, and two days into Maureen's annual summer leave, and the McLean family were ready to go off to Stirling. The 'Grand Stirling Outing' preparations had been done by Alex and his dad in the days prior to the trip. Jock had booked the coach trip and Alex had got the packed lunches ready.

Alex had received a message from STRAP telling him to take the time/space travel bag with him to Stirling, and the bag had appeared a couple of nights beforehand on his computer table. Odd, he thought, how can I possibly 'disappear' when I'm sightseeing with mum and dad and loads of other tourists? But he put it in his haversack just the same.

On the morning of the trip, Maureen was allowed an extra lie-in. She came downstairs to join them at eight o'clock to sit down to a soft-boiled egg and two croissants, her favourite breakfast, usually reserved for her birthday. This morning she was almost purring with happiness.

It didn't take much to make Mum happy, Alex thought, smiling back at her as she dropped a kiss on his head before sitting down.

In no time they were on their way, cutting down the Dalry Road to the Grassmarket. A coach came into view with the clear destination: STIRLING CASTLE showing on its front panel. They jumped aboard, all three enthused with an unexpected sense of adventure. It took just over an hour, the last stop on the trip being Stirling Castle itself. A few people had got off at the village of Bannockburn, to visit the Scottish Heritage Site first, but Jock had pointed out that if they started at the castle, the walk back to Bannockburn was downhill.

Jock and Maureen were almost the first off the

coach, with Alex scrambling after them, held up by other passengers. When he caught up with his parents, he had, for just a moment, the odd feeling that he was an intruder into their private world. Yes, this place definitely meant something special to his mum and dad.

This didn't stop Jock grumbling, though, at the exorbitant cost of entry compared with sixteen years ago.

It was a beautiful day and the castle looked magnificent in the sunshine. Just through the ticket office, the visitor was tempted by a charming outdoor cafe area, almost nestling in the battlements.

'We could just have a coffee first,' said Maureen. So, of course, they did. The three of them sat down and pored over the guide and site maps, Maureen and Jock with a coffee and Alex with a soft drink. It was clear that Maureen wanted to see the chapel, the great hall, and the artists creating the tapestries that were being newly designed as part of the palace restoration.

'I know' you'll find that boring Alex,' Maureen apologised. 'Is there anywhere you want to go?'

'Well, actually I wouldn't mind taking off on my own for an hour or so. Would that be OK? I'm more for walking round the castle walls and maybe going to see the exhibits at the Kings Old Hall.' Alex said.

Jock looked at Maureen for a decision – Maureen beamed, happy to have some time on her own, just for once, with Jock.

'Aye, Alex. You do your own thing. We can meet up back here in two hours. We can decide then whether to walk or catch the bus down to the heritage site at Bannockburn,' said Maureen.

'Thanks, Mum. I'll be back here for one o'clock. See you then.'

On an impulse, Alex walked up to the King's Old Hall. The oldest building on the site, built in 1496, it was still not old enough to have been there at the time of Bannockburn. There were rooms full of army regalia and uniforms from all periods. Alex was wandering aimlessly from room to room when his mobile started to pulse with the STRAP ring tone. He looked at the screen. It said:

Go down the passageway at the end of the room and open the door on the right.

Alex followed these instructions. The door had 'private' on it, so Alex expected it to be locked, but it wasn't. With a quick look up and down the corridor, he sneaked in and shut the door behind him. He looked down at his mobile. Korin's face appeared briefly, and then the following message:

‹Welcome to STRAP›

We are offering you a further chance to travel back in

time..

Get undressed down to your underpants, press the time/space travel bag to your stomach firmly and key in the code 10810. Remember your instructions as given previously.

When you arrive, take out the silver disc and press it to you forehead so that you will relay pictures back to us. Remember to put the silver disc and your mobile into the bag before looking round for the clothes that you will need to put on as quickly as possible.

The screen went blank for a few seconds and then the following message appeared:

‹Details of Current Travel Option›

‹Date›
May 1314

‹Place›
Stirling Castle.

‹Landing›

Near the chapel.

‹Instructions›
After getting dressed, go into the chapel and wait for a servant.

‹Identity›
Malcolm, now a squire attendant upon the Earl of Carrick..

‹Conditions›
Complicated – (so read the following several times). It is just six weeks before the Battle of Bannockburn. Stirling Castle is in the hands of the English. Lord Mowbray, loyal to the English, is in charge of the castle with an English garrison. The previous year, the castle was besieged by Lord Carrick, brother of Robert the Bruce. However, a truce was signed in 1313 on the understanding that Lord Mowbray would hand the castle over to the Scots if the English king, Edward II, didn't come up to relieve the castle by midsummer's day 1314.

‹Equipment›
Mobile phone, travel bag.

Alex read the instructions. As he came to the description of the 'conditions', he found himself wondering how it was STRAP knew all this history if their records were lost – something didn't quite add up. If he was just going back to help them collect information, why had they said in their previous message that his trips back into the past were 'helping all humanity'?

Something about the STRAP organisation was worrying him. But, despite this, he followed instructions and undressed. His heart was thumping in his chest and his mouth had gone dry. He knew that he was afraid, but he acted like an automaton following unfailingly what they had asked him to do.

He pressed the time/space bag to his middle and then keyed in the number 10810. As soon as he pressed the green button, he heard the high-pitched whine, just as before, coming nearer and nearer. Then...Nothing.

CHAPTER 10

Plotting

The ground suddenly seemed to come up hard under his feet. He was standing on a dirt path outside a small, sturdy, stone building. The fear that had gripped him just moments before had gone; he felt excitement and a strange happiness. He had arrived back in the dim and distant past that now seemed more real than the world he had just left. He looked up and squinted in the bright sunlight at an iron cross on the roof of the building. It must be the early chapel at Stirling Castle, he thought. He turned and saw that up a short slope there were some larger buildings. They must be the original hall. Looking out beyond thick stone walls he could see that the land fell away steeply, and though there was little sign of habitation, the sweep of the valley was the exact same scene he had just viewed standing next to his mum and dad.

He looked about for the clothes. Then he spotted them: they were folded neatly, just beside the half-open wooden door of the chapel. He could see a pair of flat leather boots with trailing leather thongs, dusty and mud-splattered. He picked up the pile of clothes and the boots, and peered round the chapel door. Rows of rough benches and a few grander looking chairs at the front faced a simple stone altar. On the altar, a golden cross gleamed in the dim light that filtered through the unglazed windows in the side walls. He walked in, the stone flags cold on his feet.

The clothes were much finer than the ones he had worn before. The first garment he examined was a blue tunic of light material with some kind of scalloped pattern around the neck. There was a thin leather belt, which fastened round his waist with a buckle at one side. There was a shirt, also blue, of finer material, and some kind of trousers that fitted tightly like leggings.

'Hmm posher togs than last time,' he said out loud, and then struggled with the boots, not managing to get them to stay firm on his feet until he had bound the leather thong round the sole of his foot and tied it tight at the back of his ankle.

He had hardly finished getting dressed when he heard a voice nearby:

'Malcolm, Malcolm! ...where are ye, boy?' An old man stood at the chapel door. He wore something that looked very much like a baggy sack with sleeves and rumpled leggings underneath. His hair was a matted tangle and his face half-covered by a straggly beard. He was pretty grubby all round – not a pretty sight, as his mum would say. This must be the servant identified in the travel instructions, Alex thought.

'Ah, there you are. Malcolm, it's right and proper that you are at your prayers, but you should be attending upon your lord.' He wagged a bossy finger at Alex. 'The Earl of Carrick is with Sir Philip Mowbray in the great hall, and you should be by his side.' Again the finger wag, this time almost in Alex's face; the servant was enjoying his temporary position of order-giver.

'Should I? What for?' asked Alex, trying to find out a bit more.

'What for? What for? Why you cheeky young rascal! Don't think I don't know where you are come from – plain and simple folk like the rest of us – just because you've been honoured for climbing the Rock at Edinburgh, no need to come the high and mighty.'

Oh dear, thought Alex, I've upset the old boy – best to apologise and grovel; I bet that works, no matter what century you're in.

'I'm truly, truly sorry. I didn't mean to sound cheeky.' He hung his head. 'You know it's very difficult for me to know the right thing to do as a squire.'

'Well, I expect it is, young man, coming as you did from feeding the pigs in your father's back yard to being placed at a lord's right hand. And not just any old lord, but none other than,' he lowered his voice almost to a whisper, 'the brother of our rightful king, Robert the Bruce.'

Alex understood why the old man was whispering even though there was no one around: he was in the service of Sir Philip Mowbray, who was a supporter of the English king, and so he should be as well; but, it seemed, his real loyalty was to the Scots king, Robert the Bruce. Must be like living in Chelsea and being a Man U supporter, thought Alex.

'Well, where is his lordship? And can you tell me what he wants me to do?

'Dear oh dear, lad.' The old boy shook his tangled head of hair. 'The Earl of Carrick, as I said just a moment ago, if you had bothered to listen, is in the great hall with Sir Mowbray.'

'Yes, yes, and I am to go there, and then what?' Alex thought it much better to annoy this old boy than get into the presence of the lords and not know what to do.

'Well, this is it, Malcolm – I don't rightly know. All the servants have been sent out of the hall. Only you and Ian are to be in attendance. That is what they have ordered. They have even sent out the priests, so there is no letter-writing to be done. It's something hush hush.' He tapped the side of his nose, folded his arms, and looked very disapproving of whatever it was that was 'hush hush'.

'For some reason, known only to themselves and to the dear Lord above, they are parleying between the two of them – hatching up further plots, I've no doubt. Though after the last time, the siege was lifted, so I for one am glad of all their plotting. Yes, very glad of their plotting! Plot away, sires, I say!'

Then he started laughing out loud as if he had said something very funny. He slapped his thighs and repeated.'Yes very glad of their plotting!' He went on laughing so much, Alex joined in, first to be friendly and then just because once you start laughing for no reason, everything starts to seem funny. They were like co-conspirators in a sad world that didn't know that actually everything was just a hoot. Then they both stopped suddenly and looked at each other.

'We shouldn't be laughing, should we?' said Alex.

'No lad, we shouldn't – there are those that would think we had lost our reason to even come up with a smile, but then they haven't been through the hard times; we've been through such hard times! I'll never forget that siege, no never, not as long as I live! Nowt to eat for months but mouldy bread and measly slops of soup made from nettle leaves and scraps of stringy mutton, gristle and bone.' The old boy made a gagging gesture that started Alex laughing again, it was so like what he would have done if he'd been asked to eat food like that. But the servant put a restraining hand on his arm and a finger to his lips to stop him.

While they were talking, they had been walking up the slope towards the hall, and now they had reached the large wooden door at the entrance.

The servant pushed open the heavily studded door and pulled back the thick curtain that hung across the inside.

'Watch your step, lad! Watch your step,' he whispered before ushering Alex into a large room.

Two men were sitting at the opposite ends of a table. In front of each of them was a plate with the remains of a meal and a tankard. Alex tried to guess which one of the men was Mowbray and which the Earl of Carrick. He settled on the shorter, older man, with strands of grey in his long, dark, shoulder-length hair as Mowbray. Carrick, a younger man, held himself very straight. Clean-shaven, he had strong, determined good looks. Both men had on long, richly patterned tunics, with gold chains around their necks and several heavy rings on the fingers of their hands which they both rested on the table in front of them.

Alex saw that Ian was standing a few feet behind Carrick. Like himself, Ian was dressed much more finely than when they had met before. So, thought Alex, just as the Earl of Moray had promised them, both Ian and Malcolm had been made into squires; the two had moved up the medieval hierarchy. Squires, Alex reckoned, were like medieval personal assistants – they looked after important people and were then rewarded, if all went well. Ian looked straight at Alex, and then motioned quickly to him to join him.

Alex quietly crossed the stone floor to stand beside Ian, but as he did so, the Earl of Carrick turned in his chair to speak to him.

'Well, you took your time, Malcolm. We have finished our meal some minutes ago. Where did old Isaac find you?'

'I was in the chapel, Sire,' Alex replied truthfully.

'I cannot reprimand you for that, Malcolm; we will soon need all your prayers, that is for sure, but now we have some important work for you. You and Ian must come and sit down at the table with us.'

He motioned towards two empty chairs that were placed side by side. Alex and Ian both went over quickly and sat down, looking all the while at the earl. Alex wondered if it was usual for squires to join their masters round the table – he thought perhaps not, for obviously Malcolm and Ian had not been asked to take part in the meal.

Carrick waited for a moment before starting to speak. Mowbray sat silent at the other end.

'Ian and Malcolm, you are my most trusted squires, and there is no doubt of your commitment to the cause of our king, my brother, Robert the Bruce, and so I have chosen you for a most important mission. You must learn of our plans. We, that is, myself and Sir Philip,' he held his hand out towards the man at the other end of the table, who silently nodded his agreement, 'are entrusting you with much. Can we rely on your loyalty?'

'You need have no doubts, my lord. I pledge my loyalty to you,' said Ian.

There was silence for a moment and Alex found all three of them looking at him – desperately he thought of what words he should use, for some reason feeling guilty for pledging loyalty that wasn't really his to give.

'I give you my word, my loyalty is yours.' Alex blurted out. The words sounded to him like something you would say in a Shakespearean play, but it seemed he had said the right thing because Carrick continued.

'It will surprise you to learn that Sir Mowbray, who is here in Stirling as the English king's steward and whom everyone believes is a supporter of that king, has always in truth given allegiance to the cause of my brother, Robert the Bruce; he is true to Scotland.' He paused for a moment to see if there was any reaction from the two boys.

'I am much surprised,' said Ian, and Alex could see that he was.

'And well you may be, and so would others be if they were to learn of it. The thing is, he is in a tight spot. His daughter, like my dear sister and the wife of my brother Robert, is held captive in England. Lady Mary is his only child. Sir Mowbray's wife died some years back. He longs for Lady Mary to return safely to Scotland and care for him in his declining years. Do you understand what I am saying?'

Alex and Ian both nodded.

'If Sir Philip appears to openly betray King Edward, his daughter's life might be forfeit.'

'The loss of my daughter would break my heart,' said the older man, his shoulders hunched and his face dark with anxiety and worry.

He looks, thought Alex, like a desperate man.

Carrick carried on.

'We have had information about the size of the English army that will soon be leaving Berwick-on-Tweed and marching up here to Stirling so that they can be here before the 24th of June. It is a huge army, and its purpose is to defeat my brother once and for all. They will outnumber us no matter what we do, and so we have to try to gain the upper hand by surprise and subterfuge, and by training our men as well as we can.' Again he asked: 'do you understand?' and again they both nodded.

'To gain an advantage, we have thought up this plan.' Alex remembered the old servant's words, 'plotting and planning' – how right he had been!

'You, Ian, are to ride as fast as you can to Berwick-on-Tweed. You will go to the King Edward as if you are Sir Mowbray's squire. Sir Mowbray has agreed to this, and you will tell him exactly what I am about to say to you.' Carrick looked intently at Ian.

'Yes, Sire,'

'You will say that you have come from Sir Mowbray to tell him that the Scots are planning to muster their army in Tor Wood some six miles from here. As you know, we are preparing to fight much closer to Stirling. Our army will be waiting for the English in the woods at New Park, four miles further on. Men are already digging the holes and trenches in the ground and along the road that goes through New Park to this castle. These are traps for the hooves of the horses of the English cavalry! The cavalry are King Edward's greatest weapon against us. If we can immobilise them we will have a chance. If you tell him that Robert the Bruce is planning to lie in wait at Tor Wood, once he has passed there he will bring his army along at a pace, thinking we have turned tail and so there will be less chance of anyone discerning our traps, and we can come down out of the woods at New Park upon an army in disarray.'

·Wow, thought Alex, that's pretty impressive stuff. These guys are good at this battle planning. He looked across at Ian, wondering if he was as impressed, but Ian was looking down at the table.

'You will also give him the false information that the men in Robert's army are undisciplined and wild.'

Carrick paused and looked across at Ian, who

was deliberately avoiding eye contact. Ian's face was a blank, just as it had been that day before the climb. Suddenly Alex realised that his friend was scared. What Carrick was proposing was dangerous, extremely dangerous; giving false information to the English king would mean instant death if it was found out.

Carrick went on talking for a while about the great service Ian would be doing to the Scottish people. Then he asked Ian to repeat the information he was going to give to King Edward. Ian said exactly what he had been told to say. Word perfect.

'Well, Ian,' said Carrick with forced jolliness, obviously ignoring the seriousness of what he was asking his squire to do. 'You can ride back into Scotland with the English army. You can show your loyalty and that of Mowbray by riding alongside the English knights. Goodness me, what an opportunity is that! We may be lying dead on the battlefield and you can drink and dine in style with the mighty Sassenachs!' Carrick laughed as if it was a good joke.

'Aye, a good opportunity to show everyone I had turned traitor,' said Ian. That stopped Carrick laughing.

'Ian, all of us round this table know that what

you are doing is a great service to your fellow Scots and to our cause. We know the dangers.' Carrick said nothing for a few moments and there was silence in the hall. Then he said, with a touch of menace in his voice: 'Are you unwilling to carry out this mission? Must I send Malcolm here?'

'No, Sire, you can rely on me. I am ready to do as you have bid.' Ian stood up and Carrick went over and placed an arm round his shoulder.

'God speed, Ian.' Carrick said roughly. 'Your horse is ready.'

'Is it all right, Sire, if I go to the chapel to pray first?'

'You may, of course. But ride with all swiftness. You should be in Berwick in three days.'

Ian left the hall.

'Should I leave as well?' Alex asked. He started to get up, anxious to go with Ian so that at least he could speak to him before he set off on his dreadful mission.

'No, Malcolm, stay seated, I must explain your duty. You are not so gifted with words as Ian, so you have a simpler task. Go to my brother Robert, who is marching here to Stirling, and tell him what you have heard here today.'

'Aye, Sire.'

'You can manage that, can't you?'

Oh, thought Alex, so Malcolm's the thicko is he? Is it because they know he comes from a poor family? Medieval prejudice.

'I can manage that, Sire,' said Alex, quite sure that the lord would not pick up the ever-so-slightly sarky tone in his voice.

'And mark you tell him we have already begun digging the holes and trenches that will ensnare the hooves of the English cavalry.'

'I will, Sire.'

After closing the massive hall door, Alex ran down the slope towards the chapel as fast as he could, wanting to see Ian before he left. Ian was standing in the porch and looked as if he had been waiting for him.

'My God, Malcolm, I was so glad to see you come back into the room.'

'Why?'

'You know well why – I thought you had carried out your threat to leave and go back to the village.'

'Now would I do that?'

'Malcolm, with your temper you are capable of doing anything – just like that day you marched off on me before we did the climb.

'Well it got your courage up didn't it? And it looks like you need a heck of a lot of courage now.'

'Yes, you're right. I've never felt so bad about anything as I do about this; I've got to pretend to be a traitor – my God! But you have been such a help to me these last few months, Malcolm. Living with those of a higher station is a treacherous business – give me a rock face to climb any day, rather than keep up with their double-dealing. What did Carrick ask you to do?'

'Oh my job's a piece of cake, really – I've to ride to Robert the Bruce and tell him what has been planned here today.'

'Well, nice of him to tell his brother! I realised that he had not consulted him about this. Carrick is the headstrong one. He will be thinking of the glory that would come to him if the English king comes into Scotland and they defeat him.'

'Surely the glory would come to his brother, Robert the Bruce?'

'Yes, but in battle anything can happen, Robert might be killed and then who would be king?'

'Surely you're not thinking…?'

'No, I'm not. Edward Carrick is loyal to his brother, of that I am sure. But he is desperate for Robert to be acknowledged King of Scotland by all.

Then their family will be strong, including himself. Don't forget how many of them have been killed in this endeavour, three brothers at least have died in the fighting and their sister still living in terrible captivity.'

'No wonder they want revenge! But Ian, it's you I am worried about now.'

'You know, it's strange – just a few short months ago, I would have willingly laid down my life for the cause of a Scottish King, but now I have lived so close to those of power, all I want to do is go back to the village and, if she would have me, back to the lovely Kathryn. I'm scared, Malcolm, scared I shall never return.'

Alex didn't know what to say. He had to try to say something encouraging; 'it may not turn out as bad as you think,' was all he could manage.

'My hope is that the English king will believe my story, believe that I am a traitor to the Scots in the pay of Sir Mowbray. Then I can march back into Scotland with the English army. Be one of them. Aye, seeing that my Lord Carrick cares not whether I live or die…maybe my best bet would be to fight alongside the English. After all, hasn't Carrick told us that their army is much bigger than ours? They have cavalry, archers and hundreds more knights than we have. They are going to obliterate us. I would fight to the end if I was with the Scots, but seeing that I have to play the part of the traitor, perhaps I should reap the benefits – 'what an opportunity', as my lord Carrick said.'

Suddenly Alex felt a shiver of fear run up his spine and he knew what he must say – was this why he had come back to 1314 again?

'No! Listen to me, Ian, on no account march to Stirling with the English army.' Alex stared hard at his friend, willing him to understand what he knew, and every school child in Scotland knew of the bloody battle of Bannockburn, and just who had won. 'Of course you will have to come into Scotland with them. You will have to convince them that you're Mowbray's squire and are loyal to them. But somehow, Ian, as you near Stirling, slip away before you reach the battlefield.'

'Why? Do you not think I would enjoy a handsome pay-out from the English king – perhaps my own little manor house somewhere? After all, the de Bruce family have relations in Guisborough.'

'Guisborough? Where in the world is Guisborough?'

'Across the border in Northumberland.'

'Really?' For a moment this strange bit of information stopped Alex's train of thought, but then he felt his mobile start to throb and he knew he had to be quick. 'Never mind that, Ian, just listen to me. I *know*...' he paused to emphasise the word. 'I know that you must not fight on the side of the English.'

'Oh, you know do you? Is that information from your mother's art of seeing into the future?'

'I'm not saying. Just promise me that you will not even consider it, Ian.'

'I will heed your warning, Malcolm,' Ian said slowly.

'No, you must promise me, as a friend. You must promise.' Alex repeated.

Ian grasped Alex's hand and said: 'I promise you, my good and true friend, I will not fight on the side of the English'. Then he turned quickly and went.

As soon as he had gone, Alex struggled out of Malcolm's clothes. He left them in a neat pile on the bench. Then he slipped the mobile out of the bag and keyed in 10810. He heard the high-pitched whine coming near, nearer...but then, instead of getting ear-splittingly loud as it had done before, the whine stopped. Fear stuck to the roof of his mouth as Alex glanced down at his phone. The screen was blank. He keyed in

10810 again and watched intently.

Words flashed up:

Malfunction – Malfunction – Malfunction, over and over. Then the screen went blank again.

'What do you mean, 'malfunction'? There can't be a malfunction. There can't be!' He keyed in 10810 repeatedly, only to watch the blue flashing message 'malfunction' come up again and again, and nothing else.

After several attempts that always had the same result he sat down, defeated. Ruth's words came back to him:

'Make sure you're not stuck in some weird medieval century.' And he had promised that he wouldn't be. And now he was. He had made the promise so confidently, as if he had some way of ensuring his safe return, and now there was nothing for him to do but to key in some stupid numbers that didn't work. No back up plan.

For the first time, Alex really understood the dangers of what he had agreed to do for STRAP. He imagined his mum and dad searching for him all over the Stirling Castle site, their happy family outing suddenly turning into a nightmare as no amount of requests on the public address system resulted in Alex turning up.

The police would come; people would search the countryside around the castle; it would be on the news. He would become a missing-children's statistic. Was he abducted, or did he run away? They would question his parents, his friends, his school, but there would be no trace of him. It was unbearable to think about.

And where was his alter-ego, Malcolm? Stuck in some alternative universe? He looked across at the pile of clothes that only a short while earlier he had so confidently left for Malcolm.

He heard a noise and looked up. He saw the figure of a boy silhouetted against the bright sunlight of the door. Was it Malcolm?

The boy walked towards him. Alex stood up and faced him, ready for a fight if necessary – adrenalin racing through his veins at top speed.

'It's alright – it's OK.' The boy stopped, but Alex still couldn't see him clearly. 'I've come to get you back to the 21st century.' Then Alex realised that the boy was, like him, dressed in underpants with a time/space bag stuck to his body and a mobile phone in his hand.

'Don't be scared – I know exactly what you're going through, I've been through it myself.'

'Who the heck are you?'

'My name's Danny Higgins and I live in a town just outside Nottingham.'

'Danny Higgins? I've heard that name.'

'Have you? From whom?'

'The girl who contacted me from STRAP – Korin; the first time she contacted me, she thought I was you.'

'Well I'm not at all surprised that STRAP made that mistake. They are a rogue outfit – believe you me. But we mustn't waste time chatting. Malcolm is due back into his time zone any minute now and he mustn't find us here. Use this mobile.' Danny Higgins opened his time/space travel bag and handed a mobile to Alex.

'Key in 15798 – it's my co–ordinates, but SHARP – that's my outfit – have got you programmed in on my stream just this once. I can't leave till you are back at your base. I need to follow you really quickly, so go now. Just repeat the number to me.'

'It's 15798,' said Alex.

'Great, Alex, well done! Now go, go, GO!'

Alex didn't need telling a second time. He keyed in 15798 and pressed the red button. He heard the far-distant whine getting nearer and nearer until it throbbed in his ears, and never was he more glad to have an ear-splitting sound hammering into his head…Then nothing.

He was back in the store-room. His own clothes were just as he had left them, tucked onto one of the shelves beside a pile of files. He was back in the 21st century! He got dressed quickly, tried unsuccessfully to stop himself shaking from head to toe and made his way down to the meeting place with his mum and dad.

His mum took one look at him:

'Goodness Alex, what's the matter?'

'I'm not so well, Mum.'

Maureen felt his head, took his pulse, asked him to put his tongue out and declared that Alex had got the flu. No one argued with her. They took the first bus home.

'Well, I guess we'll just have to do the Bannock-burn Heritage site on another visit,' said Dad.

Acknowledgements

I would like to thank:

My daughter Sarah Garrett and Rachel and Ethan Garrett for their support, advice and enthusiasm throughout the writing of this book.

Jane Schaffer, my publisher, for commissioning me to write the fourth Time Travelling story in her Time Traveller Kids Series, and to set it in the City of Edinburgh where I was born and brought up.

Chris Tabraham, historian, archivist, writer for giving me a full hour of his time on the telephone to answer endless questions; also to the guides at Edinburgh Castle who firmed up a key link as to where and how the Rock could be scaled on the night of 14th March 1314.

Evelyn Wilson, learning officer at the Bannockburn Heritage Site who patiently discussed the complexities of the Battle of Bannockburn and took time out to show me the most likely place she believed to be where the Scottish soldiers crossed the burn 'over the bodies of the dead' in June 1314.

Magnus Lyon, Instructor at Edinburgh International Climbing Arena and Craig Scampton, Chief Instructor of Adur Outdoor Activities Centre for their technical advice and encouragement in the sections relating to rock climbing.

I am hoping that the young people who read this book will feel drawn to training in rock climbing as this can lead to the joys, both physical and spiritual, of climbing and exploring the great outdoors in our stunning Highlands and elsewhere in the UK... Europe... Nepal... America... the World!

COMPETITIONS AND ACTIVITIES

Seven Arches Publishing often runs competitions for you to enter with prizes of book tokens, that can be spent in any bookshop, for solving puzzles or for a good illustration. Why not go to www.sevenarches-publishing.co.uk and check out whether there is competition or activity on its way based on one or other of our books. We often include the winning entries of our competitions, or the writing, poems or pictures that you send us in the next print run of the title.

CONTACT US

You are welcome to contact Seven Arches Publishing by:

Phone: 0161 4257642

Or

Email: admin@sevenarchespublishing.co.uk

Collect other books in the Time Traveller Kids series

Even though Danny's interest in history is zero, when a mysterious boy from the future tells him that he can travel back in time by pressing one of the buttons on his mobile phone, he cannot resist the challenge. Making friends with kids living in Tudor times gets him seriously hooked on time travel.

Danny has become an experienced Time traveller but this doesn't help him when SHARP's systems fail and he is left stranded in 671 when wolves roamed the English countryside.

Incredibly musically gifted, Atlanta is entranced by the music of the far-into-the- future humankind. Is this what makes her agree to join the growing band of twenty first century kids who go back in time to gather information, for the organisation called SHARP?